Get It
How You Live

Paperback ISBN 978-1-7359160-0-2
Ebook ISBN 978-1-7359160-1-9

Red Cap Books
An imprint of Red Cap Publishing LLC
66 PO Box Chattanooga, Tennessee 37437

For more information, email Books@redcappublications.com

10 9 8 7 6 5 4 3 2

Get It
How You Live
Second Edition

Tamika Bumpass

Red Cap Publishing LLC.

Text "BOOKS" to 2100 to receive release dates on upcoming books by your favorite author.
Follow on Social Media
IG @redcappublishing
Facebook Red Cap Publishing
Enjoy these types of books look for the following books.

1) "Hard Knock Life" By Tamika Bumpass coming December 2020
2) "Knee Deep In Da Game" By Tamika Bumpass coming December 2020
3) "Life With Louie" By Tamika Bumpass coming early 2021
4) "Sky's Da Limit" Ny Tamika Bumpass coming early 2021

Contents

Chapter 1
Chapter 2
Chapter 3
Chapter 4
Chapter 5
Chapter 6
Chapter 7
Chapter 8
Chapter 9
Chapter 10
Chapter 11
Chapter 12
Chapter 13
Chapter 14
Chapter 15
Chapter 16
Chapter 17
Chapter 18
Chapter 19
Chapter 20
Chapter 21

Chapter 1

"What the hell am I going out into?" Kittie's thoughts wondered as she laid on her prison bunk. Tomorrow was her max out date, and the state was throwing her out. As of tomorrow, she would officially be homeless.

For the last five years, she had lived in the state of mind the day she came in, always wondering how her life came to what it was: Worthless. And constantly reliving the dreadful day that she was charged with killing a man because she needed her a hit.

Five Years earlier...

"Ma'am, I'm sorry, but this dress has been worn. Saks 5th Avenue has a strict return policy that states any merchandise brought back into the store for a refund must be new and in a resalable condition. As an employee, I must adhere to the company's policy to the fullest. There is nothing I can do with this," the salesclerk said, nose touted, barely wanting to touch the dress as she attempted to put it back into the bag.

Before that could happen, Kittie had snatched the dress out of her hand and threw it back on the counter. "Worn. This is brand new! If it's worn, that's how I bought it."

Unconvinced, and frowning, the salesclerk held up the dress, that was soiled under the arms, with a stain on the back that looked to be a spot of period blood. "Are you serious?" The salesclerk asked in disbelief.

"Ginelle, is everything all right?" Up walked another blond hair, blue-eyed salesgirl, questioning her co-worker.

"No! Everything ain't muthafuckin' aight!" Kittie answered for the salesclerk Ginelle.

Sigh! "Well, she is trying to return this dress for a cash refund, and it has clearly been worn," Ginelle trying to be slick, on the sly, pointed out the bloodstain, but the second salesgirl- who Kittie had shaken, either didn't notice it or pretended she didn't.

"Clearly *'worn'*? Wore by who? *'me'* or *'you'*? You ain't seen me in this shit- so it musta been wore by yo' sneaky ass, and I bought it without noticing it! Now you wanna give me problems "bout something you done? Yo ass fool-up!" Kittie was now screaming while looking into the second salesclerk's eyes. She was causing an embarrassing scene, and all the salesclerk, who had turned beet red from terror, could do was nod her head like she was in agreement with Kittie.

"Ginelle, I don't know what to tell you," she said, and as quick as she got in Kittie's business, she got out. "I have customers to attend." She mumbled, not being heard as she hurried off back to her area.

"Well, I'll just have to call a manager," Ginelle chirped.

"Yeah, you just do that," Kittie spat back, then rolled her eyes hard, while mumbling, "stupid bitch. You don't own this shit."

A few minutes later, up walked a nervous-looking white guy. "Ma'am... Can... I... Help...You?" After almost every word he said, he made a noise that sounded like a chicken's clucking.

"Can you?" Kittie looked at the man crazy, frowning while wondering what kind of dope his ass had got a hold of. "I need to return this dress! It's never been wore. It got the tags on it, and y'all return policy is the customer is always right. Satisfaction guaranteed!" She screamed.

"Well, ma'am-"

Kittie cut him off just as he made that clucking noise. "What is it? Because I'm black!" She questioned, not looking anywhere near black. With her butter pecan skin and wavy grade of light-colored hair, most people assumed she was anything but black. "Yeah, I think that's what it is. Because I'm black, I get a hard time- even though I gots my receipt. Y'all don't care about that, though. You don't want to honor your own return policy, just cause I'm black. I can't believe this shit. It's a whole new millennium and look how y'all is actin'!" Kittie ranting had attracted a crowd of watchers watching.

"They won't give you your money back, and you have your receipt?" An older black nosey customer asked.

"What?" The lady's friend gawked.

Whitey looked around at the crowd and detected that this could be a problem. "No.... that's.... not.... it...." He said, still clucking while handing her a return slip.

Kittie scribbled a fake name on the form, then was refunded three-hundred-eighty-two dollars and seventy-six cents for the skimpy Alexander Wang slip dress that she had stolen out of her sister's, Shuga, closet.

Kattie had thought that the dress was new because of the price tags that were still attached. She did not know Kresa's trifling ass (Shuga's so-called best friend) had snuck the dress, wore it, and dogged it, then put it back unnoticed. Kittie would have stolen something else from Shuga had she known all this.

Earlier, she had gone searching for anything that she knew Shuga would never miss. It was not hard to find the receipt because Kittie knew since Shuga was a little girl, she was borderline OCD and stayed obsessed with being organized. So, she kept them neatly put up in a box. Kittie ran out of the mall and jumped on MARTA's bus line in route to Joe's!

Her dealer!

Kittie took the bus to the King Memorial train station to get back on the other side of town. As she anxiously waited for the train, she paced side to side; out the corner of her eye, she caught a couple just staring at her.

Kittie hated when folks looked at her judging her as if like they were better than her. Shit pissed her off. She might have been a little raggedy on the outside, but on the inside, she knew who she was.

Mad, she thought back to a pivotal moment in how her life got to this point.

"What's the use? She does not do nothing but lie!"

Kittie looked on, rolling her eyes with attitude as her latest foster mom talked about her like she was not even there. Not like that was anything new or different for her to act like anyone of the foster kids existed. But normally, whenever they had visitors in the home, she was always super fake and doling over them like she loved them so much or even liked them a little.

Which in return, Kittie was fake too. Quick and early, she learned she had to do what she had to do to get what she needed, and at this point, what she needed more than anything was to make sure she looked out for her sisters and to make sure they stayed together.

"Ms. Lyle-Green, I still need to talk to-"Interrupting the social worker, "Talk to her! To listen to lies...." She was clearly ruffled; as she talked, her always

kempt slicked back bun was disheveled, and with her every movement, more pieces became untucked.

"Ms. Lyle. Green. Regardless. If. She. Say. It's. Raining. Gold. I. Must. Speak. With. Her." *The social worker said through clenched teeth. "I must investigate this. Anytime a teacher feels a situation is serious, we are contacted to handle it. I, as a childcare worker, must fully investigate. So, if you don't mind, I'd like to conduct this interview now. And you can leave us alone."*

"You might not want to trust being alone with the little lying bitch," Kittie's foster mom mumbled under her breath, but the social worker had heard her.

Ms. Smith, the DFACS social worker, looked at the pretty little girl in front of her and wondered what the sadness was that her sharp green eyes held.

Kittie, using her defense mechanism, which was rolling her eyes hard and with much attitude, assumed Ms. Smith was just like all the other adults that had graced her life, starting with her own mom.

Kittie hated when she thought of her mom because always without warning, a sadness that she could not control always overtook her and she hated showing emotions. To Kittie, showing feelings was only a sign of weakness. No matter what was done to her, now, she learned not to let anyone feel that they had gotten the best of her.

At nine years young, Kittie had seen and sometimes experienced more than most people take to their grave.

So, as this bitch sat in front of her trying to pretend, she cared or even better that she was her friend like her fake ass teacher had done, then turned her in... She knew they had to get out of state custody, and from that night, she and her sisters were on their own.

Kittie looked down at herself; outside of her dangerous habits, she could have been a perfect ten. She was hi-yellow with green eyes, and as much damage as she kept doing to her body, it was still tight. Left in the train station were only her, a geek monster, and a lady who looked too young to have so many kids tagging along behind her. The geek monster stood scoping. Kittie knew the look he held in his eyes, but she did not understand why he had it lasered at her. She knew she did not look like she had money, cause his eyes signaled: *He ready to do whatever for his fix!*

"What the fuck you looking at me for nigga? I ain't got no muthafuckin money. I ain't got but seventy-six cents to my name." Continuing to bluff him, she dug the change out of her pocket, steady talking shit. "What you want this? Go get yo' stankin ass a job! You junkie muthafucka! With yo-" Before she could finish her sentence, he had run over and snatched the change out of her hand without dropping any and without breaking his pace. "You sorry ass bastard!" She screamed out but knew better than to run after him.

She should have known not to tempt no junkie with some money. She knew firsthand what they will do in a quick minute because she knew what she would do in a quick minute. If you got it, she was gone, take it for hers.

Kittie made it to Joe's and busted in the door like she owned the place. "What up! What up! What up!" She shouted, dancing around.

"N'all, Kittie, you ain't welcome 'round here," Turk said, thinking back to the last time he had seen Kittie about two months ago. She had been at the trap for days straight, sucking and fucking anything that came through with a hit. After four days of this, unknown to anyone at first, she ended up overdosing. One of the dirty dick niggas that had kept her high thought she just wanted to sleep. For her not getting her tired ass up, he beat her, not knowing she was unconscious nobody gone play him out of his shit. Turk stopped it and because he did not want no dead bodies at their shit. He dumped her body in the parking lot at Grady hospital. He thought she would die there, but here she was back at it, pulling more tricks out of her bag, acting like she was the cat with nine lives.

"Gone now, Kittie!" He screamed.

Apparently, she did not think he was talking to her, and if he was, he was not serious, cause she kept right on walking in the house.

"I said you ain't welcomed here!"

"What you mean welcomed? Since when do a muthafucka get on a list for invitation to a muthafuckin' trap? Tell me where's the fucking welcoming committee, cause I gots to sign up..." She rolled her eyes. "Dumb ass nigga! Just do what you do and serve me up." She said, waving two hundred dollars back and forth, smiling, showing her neon yellow-colored unbrushed teeth. She assumed with him seeing the sight of her with money, he was gone forget about what had happened the last time.

"N'all, Joe told us we can't take yo' money and can't nobody serve you." Turk shook his head, adamant. He was obeying all of Joe's orders.

"Joe said that? What!" Kittie pretended to be hurt. "Well fuck Joe."

"Shit, man! Just gone, leave! Damn!" He said, mad now as he threw the remote to the Xbox 360° game he had just lost. Kittie did not move. "Gone now! Shit! Just get the fuck on!

Kittie was not going nowhere. She must have thought she was at Burger King, where customers get it their way. Today, she was not getting served, and Turk was sticking to that. She was not seeing it, though.

"Bring yo' ass on," he said, pulling her shoulder toward the door.

"Fuck n'all nigga! I ain't going no muthafuckin' where! Shit! Drug dealers with fucking integrity? Fuck that! Just serve me up, cause I ain't going nowhere, shit! .... I ain't leaving! What you gone do? Call the po-po? Tell 'em I'm trespassing," she laughed. "Tell 'em whatever the fuck you like, but I ain't going nowherrrreeeee!"

Turk had scooped her up from the knees, backwards she fell hard with her head ricocheting against the concrete, then he drugged her little 98- pound body out the door. She was trying to kick and fight her way free. But since she had threatened him on the sly with that police shit, he was not going to spare her and be gentle. She held onto the money tight as he threw her down the steps of the porch, following her, he gave her a kick straight up her ass. She winced, feeling the blow all the way up her spine.

From the ground, Kittie continued her shit-talking, "You black tall skinny skelator-looking muthafucka! Just wait! Just wait! I' ma get some dudes and have yo' ass touched!" She coughed out.

"Bitch, listen to yo 'self. You a 'J'! Don't nobody fuck with yo' stankin' ass." Turk laughed and snatched her money. He turned and spit a mucus-filled wad of spit right on the side of her face.

Kittie laid there in the dirt, then numbly got up and walked straight to Turk's Camaro. Under the passenger's seat, she found what he kept hidden. Dreamlike, she made it up the steps, through the door, and back in the house, where Turk was back playing Hate It or Love It by 50 cent featuring. The Game. Oblivious to his surroundings, he was startled when he heard a click, jumping; he turned to see his own 9 aimed down at him.

"Kittie. Damn, man here," he said, pretending to dig in his pocket.

In one swift movement, he had grabbed her arm and twisted it around, thinking that the pain would cause an instant drop of the gun.

Instead, the gun went off.

The bullet went into the wall.

"Damn bitch you crazy," he screamed as she still held the gun tight. He pulled her fist closer to bite her, so she would let the gun. She felt his teeth tear into the flesh of her middle finger. A single tear of pain escaped as part of her finger fell with the gun, she screamed. At the same time, the gunshot again.

Kittie looked down and saw that Turk's old ass gun with the hairpin trigger had gone off again. This time shooting Turk in the chest.

Looking at the quickly forming puddle of blood, Kittie snapped back into reality. Seeing everything around her, but unable to think, she did not know what to do.

"Turk? Turk, you alright?" She just dropped the gun and ran out the door when silence was all she got as an answer.

Eventually, she was tied to the murder when the police got the call about the body and fingerprinted the gun. The prints came back belonging to Kateria Mason, better known around the way as Kittie. The police then charged her with first-degree murder, but later through a plea bargain, the district attorney dropped it down to manslaughter and gave her five years of prison time.

Present Day...

Today, Kittie stood at the gates nervously, waiting for them to be opened so that her release from prison would be complete. Once through them, she would be back in the free world. All alone and not knowing what she was about to face. Kittie did not know where she was going or what she was going to do once she found a place to go to. Her counselor at the prison had given her information on a women's shelter for substance abuser, just because it was part of her job, not that she cared about Kittie's success rate.

Finally, she walked through the last gate, shoulders slumped, and head down with the directions in her head along with a thirty-five-dollar check that was issued to all inmates upon their release. The check was supposed to help them gain access into society and help them with a fresh start... Thirty-five dollars? What the fuck could she do with thirty-five dollars? She started in the direction of the bus line.

A horn blew in the distance. It could not have been for her, though. No one even knew she was getting out of prison today.

"Kittie! Why the fuck is you just walking? Where the hell is you going?"

It was Shuga. She had stepped out of her car, looking like a chick straight off the TV screen. Her golden skin glistened as her long jet-black hair blew behind her. Her chiseled facial features belonged on the cover of magazines... Maybe not the classy kind, but at least the trashy kind.

Shuga was beautiful but very intimidated by Kittie's natural beauty. While growing up, Shuga played a major role in Kittie's very low self-esteem. Shuga always had to be the most or have the most. She would have done that Shit to Bree, their younger sister, but she was not having that.

"Hey auntie," Mineta, Shuga's six-year-old daughter, skipped over, looking like if Kittie had a daughter, this would be her.

"The last time I saw you, you was in diapers," Kittie smiled. "Do you remember me?"

"No," Mineta answered. "But as soon as my Mom Shuga pointed at you standing by them gates, I knew who you was. Cause everybody say I look like you. But they say if I start acting like you, they gone beat my ass." She put a hand on her nonexistent hip, smiling, revealing two missing teeth. Shuga walked up.

"Too damn late! With yo' fast ass! I heard what you said. I swear this child is you reincarnated!"

"Let's hope not!"

"Hello." They hi-fived each other, then Shuga grabbed her sister, "I am so glad that you are out of that place. You look really good." Kittie looked - it was not Shuga's usual style to commitment anyone. "I'm serious, you look good. Like one of them, thick cornbread fed girls from Alabama. Hoes is paying for these shapes." She rubbed a hand down her own curvaceous figure, putting the shine right back on herself. "These niggas is gone; wonder where the hell this light skin thick redbone came from. They'll never guess its Kittie."

A slight mention of Kittie's past had her on edge. "Yeah, well, I'd like everyone to forget that, Kittie. Can we get outta here?"

"You in a rush to leave now? Good! You might think twice about doing some bullshit to go back... So, Kittie, the oldest sister, has matured, huh?" Shuga asked once they were in the car.

"My God, yes! That's a jungle in there. That shit worse than Techwood."

Techwood- where they lived before being sent into foster care- was considered the worst, most violent anything goes project in Atlanta. It was the first project to be torn down during Atlanta's reconstruction.

"Damn, well, we gone call you Kat since you ain't that young dumb Kittie no more."

"Yeah, I don't care. I ain't trying to go back to nothing I used to know."

"Good! Just remember you said it."

"This a nice ass car!"

"Bitch, I know! It's a 2010 Dodge Charger," Shuga bragged.

"2010?"

"Yeah!"

"But, it's only 2009!" Kittie said, looking lost and feeling the world had left her behind.

"I know," Shuga said proudly.

"So, what are you doing? Where you work?"

"Work? Come on with the games! You know Shuga don't damn work! I'm still fucking with these niggas heads while emptying their pockets. You know I got it like that. I would've gotten a Benz. I could have, but this nice without all that extra attention. Ya, feel me?" Shuga winked, then turned to look at Mineta, who had been all in her mouth. "I'm dropping yo' I 'm-so-sick-cough-cough-ass at school. School ain't even been in a good month, and you already missing all kinda days, faking not to go."

On cue, Mineta started her fake cough, "Shuga, I is sick. Hear me?"

"No, I don't. Yo' auntie need some clothes and you ain't finna tagging along everywhere. You see what she got on?"

"Yes, I do. Did you see those shoes?" Mineta asked, grown like she knew the style.

Chapter 2

"Shitted on 'em! Shitted on 'em! Shitted on 'em! Put ya number two's in da air if you did it on 'em. You bitches ain't fucking with me!" Shuga rapped loudly, along with Nicki Minaj, while she stunted on all the neighborhood hoes, pulling up in her brand-new candy apple red Dodger Charger.

"Bitches hate! That's right, cause I'm the shit!" Shuga said, while still rocking, as the bass boomed out of the custom subwoofers.

"Shuga! Shuga!" Shawan ran out her front door holding her hound dog titties.

'Ignorant bitch, shoulda been embarrassed walking around without a bra like she a perky 32A, instead of a pancake-shaped 50Z. Bitch know she need a bra all-day-everyday.

Shuga would never be caught stepping out of the house like that. Better yet, Shuga would never be caught stepping around in the house like that. Automatically, the left side of Shuga's lip crooked in disgust.

"Shuga, spot me a five till I can get to the store to get this money off my EBT card," she waved the card in the air.

"A five? As in five dollars?" Shuga questioned.

Shawan nodded her head up and down like a puppy.

Shuga stepped outta her ghetto Benz. "Didn't I just see James creeping up out ya place, this morning and here you is asking me for five dollars? I'm lost."

Shawan had waited on Shuga all day, and this was not the reaction she wanted but should have expected. "It ain't like I'm asking you to give me shit. All I need is for you to loan it to me until I can get to the store, bitch! But since you wanna act all grand and siddity, never mind!"

"Hoe, I ain't the one begging so you damn right-never mind! And know this, you wasn't gone get it no way."

"If it wasn't for all them niggas you wouldn't have shit either," Shawan spit at her.

"Hold-up, cause you damn right. I ain't the one to suck nor fuck for free. I gets mine. You see how my ass is all reclined, comfortable in this soft butter leather. That's right bitch get like me," Shuga said, then gyrated her wide hips into her apartment, leaving Shawan stupid ass looking-well stupid.

Shuga did not have time to even give hoes like Shawan further thought. She had shit to do like collect mo' money. She was one to always stick to the motto, *'if it don't make money, then it don't make cents.'*

Today was the first of the month, and everyone knew what that meant, especially Shuga.

Bills due!

Not that she had any real bills. No, nothing like that. Shuga lived in the Atlanta Overlook, which was not nothing but a remodeled project, but if you were blindfolded and was guided to her place without seeing the outside, then stepped up in her shit, no one could guess. Not when your feet sunk into thick posh rugs, with paint and wallpaper on the walls. Throughout her shit, it was laid. For her, it was easy to do because she lived virtually rent-free. The place included some utilities and went by one's income. Which, to them, she reported as zero. Never telling the gossiping, lifeless caseworkers, whose noses' stayed up in hers, her baby daddies name, they could never take a percentage out of her welfare check or food stamps when they went to collect child support. Shuga just played the part of the average black girl in urban America; *'I do not know who my baby daddy is!'*

So that was that! Shuga did not care how she appeared to people who could do nothing for her. The state would not getting commission off of her. She could collect her own money, and that is what she did like clockwork, three to ten hundred dollars from each of her three baby daddies for her one child.

That is right, one child!

During the time Shuga got pregnant, she had slept with multiple men. She could not accurately pinpoint whose sperm had fertilized her egg. It was a shame, but she really did not know who had fathered six-year-old Mineta. So, without further ado, or causing herself anymore, stress on the matter... Seeing a lucrative opportunity to make some dollars, they all became the child's father.

And Mineta was growing up, being taught to be just like her scheming momma, as young as she was, she knew not to talk about her daddies with the other daddies...

Shuga pulled up in front of Mary Lin elementary school, honking her horn. She had already spotted Mineta, who had one hand on her hip and the other in some nappy-headed little boys face.

"Mineta!" Shuga screamed. She had shit to do and was not about to waste a second on Mineta and her drama.

"Shuga? That you?" Mineta asked, still running to the car, not knowing if it was her or not. "Ohh, everybody get to see our new car! Yeah!" She jumped in and started pushing buttons.

"Stop fucking with shit!" Shuga yelled.

But Mineta had already stopped to hang out the window, making sure she was seen in her new car. Shuga flew off, not caring.

Rolling down Old National Highway, Shuga looked over in the First and Ten parking lot and saw Be-Be's grape splash colored bubbled eyed Chevy Caprice, and took notice of his passenger seat. In it posted was the white chick, Toni, that folks had said he was messing with, but he constantly denied.

Shuga's face took a life of its own; with the mug, she shot at them. Jealously invaded her heart as she rushed into the airtight space next to his car. She knew when Mineta opened the door that she would do major damage to the fifteen-thousand-dollar custom paint job that he bragged about to any and all of those who would listen. He was a show type nigga that always wanted his shit on display.

"Shuga! Pull yo' car over a little! Shuga! Damn! Shuga! Pull back out! You gone hit my doo-" Oops too late. Mineta had half jumped out.

"Hey, daddy!" She jumped, rocking, pushing the door about four times into the side of his car so she could squeeze herself out of the tight jam. Shuga's lively light, innocent brown eyes, smiled malice, knowing that his custom grape paint job was fucked.

Be-Be's frown instantly turned into a smile at the sight of his daughter. Mineta had his hair... He guessed. But that was about it! She was a hi-yellow little girl with a wide mouth and unruly red wavy hair. She was destined to be a knockout. Who wouldn't be proud of her? Be-Be took better care of her than of any of his real kids. He praised her for her beauty.

"Come, mere baby," he said, grabbing Mineta up.

Shuga stepped out fly girl style and twisted her wide hips to where they were standing at the trunk of the cars, all while eyeing Toni, who was in the mirror applying globs and globs of lip gloss to her thin line lips. "Here 'Neta," she said, handing her a Hersey's chocolate bar that she had wanted back at the gas station but wasn't allowed to eat in Shuga's new car.

Mineta tore into it, as Be-Be went inside his truck- pulling out what looked like a whole new wardrobe. She had clothes like a teenager instead of a six-year-old. Always the latest brands and always with the accessories to match. Shuga pushed a button on her keychain, popping her trunk for the clothes.

"Um-um," Shuga cleared her throat, once the transfer of the last bag was complete. She stood with her hand extended palm side up in the universal, give-me-my-money pose.

"Aight," he said but did not move.

"I gots to go! Ain't nobody finna play with yo' ass. You play with her!" Shuga said all loud and alley, as she pointed right at Toni, who had snapped her neck around to let Shuga know she had heard her.

"Damn! Shawty-man, why you rushing? I barely get to see her," Be-Be snapped.

"Don't shawty-man me! You know my name... Shit'd, why am I rushing? Nigga please!" Shuga could barely believe the bullshit dripping out this nigga mouth. Then again, she could.

Just look at the shit he did. She rolled her eyes, thinking of all the dumb shit. "Cause I got shit to do! I can't ride around flossing all-day long-playing house like you do! This little money you give me be gone in no time. We is in a recession... Or did you know that? Cause this barely buys her enough milk to go with her cereal...

"Maybe if yo' ass had to struggle like regular folks with a nine to five, you'd see how it is. Cause right now yo' ass gots it too easy. Yeah, yo' ass getting by too good... And it ain't my fault you don't see her. Anytime you call for her, I have her ready... When the last time you called? You call all them hoes you be with more than you check up on your own daughter." Again she said that loud just so Toni's pink ass could hear. She was trying to start some shit, for Be-Be disrespecting her by bringing his hoe with him while he handled family business. But Toni was scary, just sitting there as her man was roasted.

"Uh-" He stuttered. She did not let him finish. She was not hearing no excuses.

"Right nigga, cause this ain't no family reunion," Shuga had had it with Be-Be's wanna-be-ballin'-for-show-ass. All the money he tricked off on all those simple hoe's, she felt should have went to her. And that was the reason she done his ass the way she did him. He was a chump, and as long as he let her, she was not gone stop.

He handed her five crisp one-hundred-dollar bills, from a wad of all the same. She took the money and sighed. She just stared at him with lips poked out. He handed her another hundred.

"Give your daddy a hug, so we can be out," she said, eyeing her daughter.

Mineta quickly grabbed her 'daddy,' leaving her messy chocolate fingerprints on the back of his linen slacks. Without noticing, Be-Be jumped back inside his ride, right on his Vanilla colored suede seats.

'Simple ass nigga,' Shuga thought outraged. "Get a little money and wanna spend it on a cracker!' With that, Shuga took messy hand Mineta inside the sports bar to clean her up. There was no way she was making a mess in her new Dodge Charger.

Head high and hair bouncing, Shuga twisted back to her car, getting attention from two men who had just pulled up in work uniforms, and looked to be on their lunch breaks. Too bad they were regular working men, cause Shuga did not do that type.

She was to Hollywood for the regulars. She rolled her eyes as one of the men tried to get her attention... *"Yeah, right!"*

She looked at her dash and saw she was running late for her next meeting with Scott. Doctor Kirkland Scott!

During an unexpected mishap, she had met him one day at the clinic when she had went in for a check-up thinking she'd contracted some type of STD. In the elevator, she noticed him staring. What she noticed was his Emory hospital white jacket with Dr. Scott wrote big and glittery.

She knew she was able to snag him. A sugar daddy was long overdue for her. Then when she came up pregnant, she led him to believe he was the father. Shuga allowed him to name Mineta because she came out clearly, looking like neither him nor her. But never once has he questioned her authenticity.

She pulled into the McDonald's, and Mineta jumped out, wanting to run to the playground.

"Shuga, can I play? I wanna go play now!" She winced.

Shuga rarely denied her daughter anything, due to her own insecurities stemming from her childhood, causing her dysfunctional parenting methods, but right now, they were on a mission.

"Mineta, I'll take you to play later. Come on, yo' daddy has to get back to the hospital," Shuga said, as she took notice to a big purple swollen bump that stood out among its millions of sister and brother bumps that were spread ubiquitously on his blistered face, but that particular one appeared to be leaking goo shit. Shuga's thoughts of how he needed to go fuck something to get rid of them shits were interrupted when Mineta bounced over.

"Daddy!" She acted so happy, hugging him.

He held her hand as they walked to Shuga's car. He handed her a bank envelope with ten one-hundred-dollar bills.

"Look!" Shuga popped and got her ghetto voice. The one that was loud and alley and that she knew he hated.

"This ain't even gone be enough! Look," she popped her trunk. "Do you see all this shit I had to go buy your daughter?" She asked him, lying with a hand on her hip while extending the other. "Un-un! This ain't gone even be enough!" She got louder.

"I bring no more cash on me," he in his heavy African accent said. Shuga tilted her head, folded her arms, and poked her lips out, being stubborn. "Well, does she need anything else?" He asked lamely.

"Does she?" Shuga was taken aback. Why would he ask something like that? If she did or did not, it did not matter Shuga was gone always say she never had enough. "You know she does! Shit! She a growing child. Look how big she getting." Lies, all lies, cause Mineta was not getting big. "She barely wear her clothes three weeks, and they threw." She lied more. Not only did she want everything she saw, but she taught Mineta that same trait: To be greedy and thirsty all the time too! He dug into his pocket, pulling out his wallet, and produced a platinum American Express card.

"Well, take her to the mall and drop the card back off and I'll have you more cash," he said; Shuga almost scratched his hand up as she snatched the card out of it. Sure, she would take Mineta to the mall.

"Come on, baby," Shuga was all smiles from there out. Mineta ran and dived in the front seat.

One more stop...which, she was tempted to pass up. She really did not want to fool up with Mark or his predictable bullshit. But for Shuga to pass up money was like a booster going in a store and actually spending some. It just was not happening!

Besides, she had already spotted Mark's outdated Cadillac.

Who in the ATL is doing a bent up 78 Seville? It is about to be 2010. She got behind him and followed him to the Old National Flea market, glad she had left when she did, or he would have seen her and Scott and busted her shit wide open. He was already the biggest hater that she had ever seen. He had just stopped following her around, watching and stalking and shit... She hoped.

To this day, every time she looked at him, she regretted that she had ever gotten involved with his dusty ass. And every time her first mind warned her to leave him alone. The lure of his change and I mean change, along with her greed, kept her coming back. Dude had some serious issues! Shuga knew this- he could probably get a check. Ole boy was not wrapped tight... yet, and still, Shuga took his money.

She decided she was going to have to really consider meeting everybody on different days or locations further or something. Things were getting to close for comfort... then again, that is what she liked. The excitement of playing these niggas.

She thought she was the shit. That she was the top player in this game, and absent of any doubt, she knew no one was better. Especially with the niggas she had tricked, all top shelf, well exception being Mark's broke ass, of course.

But see, originally, he had her fooled when she had met him at the carwash in his Range Rover, doing it, one sunny afternoon. She did not find out until after she had already told him that she was pregnant, that he was broke, and that the truck was his baby cousin. By then, she was already stuck with his dramafied wo not let go ass. Once to get rid of him, she had thrown out there that the baby might not be his.

He did not like that shit, nor did he really care because he just wanted to have a part of Shuga. The fool had replied to that saying, he wanted to meet the other nigga so they could go take their blood test on the Maury show and see what was what. Cause in his gut, he just felt the baby was his. With all that bullshit he was talking, she dropped it.

"Hey baby," Mark said, getting out. His attention was on Shuga- her nose flared. This is why she hated doing this.

"Your daughter's right here," she nodded her head towards Mineta.

"Hey Mika"

"Mineta!" she screamed. "Damn! Don't you know your own child's name?" Upset, she pretended but was really shooting rockets on the inside, happier than a two-dollar hoe who'd been given a ten for her services, that he'd fucked up and called Mineta the wrong name. That gave her the reason to show the attitude that was already there. "Mika is one of your other kids; you don't take care of either! Where is her money?" She said, holding out her hand.

"Aye, listen."

"Oh, fuck nigga no!" Excuses and lies! She was about to pull off on his sorry ass. She did not need to waste no time bullshitting with this wanna-be ass muthafucka.

The only one that came with problems. Time after time and time again. Even after she had worked with his ass. She had set him up on a payment plan of only three hundred dollars a month. Three hundred dollars! Come on now!

Three hundred dollars a month for a child that could have been his was not a lot in the present day. Cause if she would have went through them white folks, his ass would have been paying way more or either in jail by now. Probably the latter.

"N'all don't aye-muthafuking-listen nothing. I don't want to hear not one excuse. If you ain't got her money, that's fine! It's okay. I ain't doing it with your sorry ass no mo'. Child Support will be contacting yo' black ass," she bluffed.

"Baby, it ain't nothing like that," he said, knowing he knew that the child support people would make him get a real job. A task his lazy ass just could not seem to function. He barely wanted to let the money go. Shuga had to snatch the bills, then she put the car that had never been turned off in reverse.

"Hold-up!" He screamed.

"What?"

"I was gone see what you was doing later. Maybe we can kick it," he was smiling all hard, showing off those crooked gapped front teeth that had started to rot.

Shuga was not gone entertain this. She did not even respond. Bastard! He knew before even asking that was not one single thing up with them.

"Bitch!" He screamed. Shuga looked in her rearview mirror and saw he was hopping. Her tires must have gotten his bad foot. She laughed as her phone rung.

It was her younger sister, Bree. She had called earlier needing to talk, but Shuga had shit to do, and all things besides that would have to wait.

Right now, she was on her way to the Lenox Square mall, Phipps plaza, and anywhere else she could think of for a shopping spree courtesy of the good doctor.

Shuga felt no type of remorse as she floated in store after store, buying shit she did not need at her daughter's expense. She even bought a four thousand-dollar Emilio Pucci dress, knowing she did not have nowhere to wear it. Shuga sauntered out the mall, feeling everything that she had bought was due to her and more.

Chapter 3

"Oh! My! God! Did you see that?" Bree's already big brown eyes were wide in amazed terror.

"Yeah! That was like totally fucking awesome, dude," Todd screamed.

Bree frowned at Todd's too excited happiness. They had just witnessed a car flip over the median divider of Interstate 285 and get chopped in half by an 18-wheeler. Everything to Todd, no matter what it is, was always *'totally fucking awesome.'*

Todd was a surfer straight from sunny California who had come to the A to attend Georgia Tech. What Bree saw in him was unknown to all that knew them. They were total opposites in every way imaginable. She was Egyptian black, and he was a tanned Ken doll. Maybe the attraction came because since Bree was a little girl, everyone had always called her black barbie. So, she had to go out and get a Ken doll. And whoever seen a real-life black Ken? So, she dated white boys. They were stuck in traffic formed from the aftermath of the crash, blasting a Nine-Inch Nails' song. Todd was headbanging while Bree was bored, looking out the window as a souped-up crept next to them. The driver was a peanut butter skinned dude with a mouthful of platinum teeth and long dreadlocks that were platinum on the tips.

"What up, shawty?" He said to Bree, who was just staring, but she couldn't hear because of their loud tremble and his loud bass, but she still waved 'cause she knew he was speaking.

Slowly, she turned to see what Todd was doing. Still headbanging. She turned back to dude.

"What's up?" She smiled and did not know what else to say. Her and this Ken doll had been together for a while now, confessed their love to one another, and had planned to be married, but slowly things were fading. They used to do everything together, but now they did nothing!

Why? Cause he was always broke and could not afford to do nothing with her if she was not paying. He barely had enough money for gas. She could not keep up with how many times they had run out and had to walk. Talk about embarrassing. She only put up with it because she had fallen in love. He was totally different from what she saw in her past. So desperately, she grasped onto everything that was unlike her past. She knew she would never be like her sisters...running through dope boys...then get turned out like Kittie.

Bree wanted so much more outta life. That is the reason she stayed in school and got her high school diploma. That is why she was on her way to having a college degree. She wanted more.

Even if she were going just to be a teacher, it was a profession and could land her a professional (man) whenever she woke up and realized Todd was not up to helping her achieve her goals in life.

Bree gave the dude one last smile, then looked straight ahead, determined not to look in his direction anymore.

She knew the type she was looking at nothing but a bad boy and getting mixed up would only bring her down. She folded her arms across her chest as Todd brought her out of her thoughts. He was yelling, holding his head.

"Whooaa! A little dizzy there... Cool!" He said, then started banging his head against the steering wheel again.

She frowned; she was so tired of his reckless tactics. She looked over at the dude, well through her peripheral view, she was too shy to actually turn and face him and saw he was on his cell phone.

Right then, the car made its familiar clinking noise. They were out of gas, stuck in the middle of a car pile-up on the busy interstate.

"No! No! No!" She could not do this with Todd no more. Frustrated, still screaming no, she jumped out the car lamely in a jean shirt, beige pants, and penny loafers that actually had the copper penny in them. Todd had found them at a yard sale and thought they were perfect when they were Bree's size.

"Excuse me. Can you give me a ride?" Bree had walked to the stranger that had been in traffic with them for hours. Bree did not know what had gotten into her, but she knew she could do bad by herself. She felt an awkward stage coming over on; her underarms had even started to sweat. Nervously, she smiled, revealing a deep dimple in her chocolate cheek. Their eyes locked, and he thought she looked like a pre-surgery Janet Jackson... Just flawlessly beautiful!

They were so lost in the moment that they had not noticed Todd's weird ass. He, too, had walked up with a sour expression on his face.

Absentmindedly, he one hand rubbing his blond hair. "Dude! Well, like, are you going to take us to the gas station?" He held up the can he carried for times like this.

Bree could not even look up; she was so humiliated. She put her face in her hands and could not believe what was happening in her life.

That was five years ago, and right now, all she wanted to do was run into the arms of the man that had saved her that day, as she walked head held high, refusing any hater the satisfaction of seeing her show any type of emotional breakdown. She wanted to glance back and steal a peek at the looks she had left the group with when she had jumped up and told everybody in the meeting to kiss her ass... All she had worked for. Gone. She believed had she not been pregnant, she had probably pulled up her skirt and given the 3D version of what she really meant.

DeKalb county's board of education had voted to suspend her teacher's license instead of getting her the proper help she needed, due to several allegations of her pinching her students, cursing her students, then the ultimate draw came when one student reported she'd spit in his face. The little boy with his bad disrespectful ass had called her a black bitch. She had run out of the classroom that day a few months back so angered behind that bullshit cause if she had not left, she probably would have hooked with his little ass. As she drove away from the school still upset, she did not even see the raggedy Ford Focus that she collided into and totaled out. She knew that the folks inside of it were happy that an insured, nonstolen 2009 Lexus LS400 had hit them. Everyone in the hooptie played their parts to the T and were all taken to Grady Memorial emergency room via ambulance.

Bree was taken to the hospital too, not because she was hurt or pretending to be but because she was pregnant. The doctors had released her after a couple tests a few hours later, assuring her that she and her baby were fine.

As she drove from the meeting today that had taken everything she had worked for, she was experiencing sharp pains that were growing. She knew she could not be in labor; she was only six months. Bree wheeled Medusa, *Quent's personal bitch,* which was an 85 Chevy El Camino that he had invested over a hundred G's in, right in front of Club Hot Shot where happy hour was in full effect and just laid on the horn. She was in so much pain; she could not breathe properly.

"Breeeee!" The club's bouncer called out then rushed to get Quent.

Quent came running to a screaming Bree.

"Baby," he put his hand on her stomach. "Aye-aye calm down. Everything is going to be alright." Quent said, carrying her to his truck. "Baby, don't cry."

They pulled into the emergency parking area, and Bree emitted a pain-induced scream that sounded like murder.

"Aaaaiiirrrahhhh!" Panting, she managed to inform him that her water had broken.

"Oh shit! Oh shit! Hold on, baby girl!" Quent bounced out the truck and ran to her side.

"Quent! It hurts so bad!" She screamed with beads of sweat running down her forehead.

By the time he got to her door, the pains were so intense that she could not do anything *but* hold her breath. As soon as he picked her up to move her, she felt like she was being razored up on the insides. Going crazy, she wanted him to stop touching her. He ran in yelling for someone to help Bree. Two nurses stopped what they were doing, grabbed her up, and laid her down on a stretcher. She was delirious now as the contractions started rolling in like waves, seconds apart.

They were at the elevator when she screamed, "It's coming!"

"Do not push!" The male nurse told her.

"I 'm-I'm-I'm not!" She screamed out, breathing heavy, chest rising and falling hard, then they heard a plop.

"The baby's head is out." The female nurse informed as she cut Bree's clothes off.

"We're almost there-," Quent started, then was jolted speechless as he watched his son slide out like slime. He was stunned, but then a euphoric feeling of greatness overcast him. He had never been this happy or proud.

He had a son! Then he fainted right there in the middle of the hall, as they rushed Bree to the Triage room and the baby to the neonatal area.

"You are going to have to push the afterbirth out." A male doctor told her.

Screaming inaudibly, Bree tried to cry out the words, no, and it hurts. But did not manage. The anesthesiologist had come and put a gas mask over her face and told her to count backward from ten.

"Ten!"

She was out.

Bree woke womb-less and childless after a three-day shock.

Quent had several times tried to calm her, letting her know that everything would be fine. That they could have more kids... Only they could not.

Bree was too ashamed and scared of losing him to tell him that something had gone terribly wrong. That she was now only half a woman.

At the same time, little Quentin Jr. would have been passing, Bree had started to hemorrhage, and the doctors had to perform a life or death surgery on her: A hysterectomy.

She had never wanted kids, not that she did not like them, but because of how helpless she had always felt growing up. If anything happened to her and she was unable to raise her child... she always felt that her child's life would be a repeat of hers, and she would not wish that on no one. But now that choice was no longer hers.

She cried at the thought of how much Quent wanted this baby.

A baby would have made them complete.

How would she be able to keep him without conceiving a child for him? With her mind starting to play tricks on her, it had her thinking that was the only thing that she could offer him to make him stay. She had totally forgotten about the four years that they were a perfect couple before the pregnancy and only focused on the last six months of her life with those thoughts, she cried herself to sleep.

Later, she awoke to Quent's hand on her stomach and was slightly disgusted with him.

"Oh, baby, you up?" He said, catching her blinking her closed eyes.

Bree felt at her hair. The Rihanna inspired haircut must have looked a mess. She had sweated her perm out during the childless labor, and her hair was matted to her head. She tried to force a fake smile, her lips were so dry and chapped that she felt them splitting.

"I know I look bad."

Vanity? Their baby had just died, and the first thing she comments on was her looks. He figured she was having one of those postpartum depression episodes that he had read about.

"No, baby. You look beautiful." Quent said, hoping to bring her spirits up.

"Yeah, right!"

He leaned in and kissed her forehead. "Don't worry, 'bout it. As soon as your six weeks are up, we'll start working on another baby. By this time next year, I'll probably have a lil' man. So, don't you worry, baby, bout shit!" He kissed her crusty lips.

Distraught, it was confirmed. He did not want her. He wanted a seed. How could she not worry? There would not be no baby coming no matter how many weeks, months, or years that they tried. Bree did not know what to do. It felt like a train was in her head going round and round. Her thinking going faster than reason. She remembered a little girl, one of her students, asking if she had kids. She had liked the little chocolate girl...at first, so she answered, telling her no.

The girl then responded with, "Good! I wouldn't want you as my mommy, and neither would anybody else."

How many of her students had said they hated her? Was this punishment for being mean all those years? Bree had never contemplated that what she was doing to her students is what was done to her as a child.

Her thoughts continued to race. How was she going to have a baby? That was all she needed to know. Quent pulled his chair closer to the edge of her hospital bed and laid his head on her stomach. A gesture that was innocent to him, but was sickening her, because she knew what he was after.... something she could not provide. What was she gone do now?

Could she lose Quent?

Who could help her?

She had to turn to Shuga...

She could help her...

She would think of something...

She always did!

***

When Shuga got the news, she came running for once, thinking of someone other than herself, with Kat and Mineta in tow. The fact was Shuga was not thinking, but Kat was.... About the reaction Bree would have upon seeing her. They had not seen each other in years since Bree was a junior in high school. Kat had written Bree a couple times while she was still in prison to never get a response. She only did it because Shuga had lied, claiming Bree said she missed her.

Later, when Kat would ask why Bree had not responded back, Shuga made excuses for Bree, with her being busy with her college work and all. So, finally, Kat gave up writing her.

"Come on, y'all!" Shuga screamed, holding the elevator open for Mineta, who could not walk fast because of her short legs that took short steps, and Kat, who dragged because she did not want to speed this reunion up. "Ooh, maybe we should got some balloons," Shuga thought aloud.

"For what?" Kat asked drily.

"Oh, yeah, that's right."

"Shuga, so why her baby died?" Mineta questioned, her big green eyes glistening, wanting to know.

"I don't know, baby. I don't know."

"Auntie Kat, do you?"

"No, Mineta, baby."

They got off the elevator, and Shuga rushed, looking for the room, finding it, then disappearing inside. Kat followed behind Mineta, who had turned to her right before they made it to the room. "I don't wanna go in there with no dead baby."

"No, the baby's not going to be in there, only Bree."

"Oh! Girl, I was bout to say!" Mineta said, grabbing at her chest, always dramatic.

Bree and Shuga were already in a conversation. Bree's mouth was gone a hundred miles an hour, until she spotted the prodigal sister, causing her talk to halt.

Bree stared at Kat.

Complete silence. But its always been said the calm before the storm.

"Quent, this is our older sister Kat," Shuga said in the eerie quiet room.

"What's up?" He nodded and already knew the deal.

"Hey, Bree. Are you okay?"

Ready to erupt, breaking her stare down, she snapped.

"No! I'm not okay. I just lost my baby. Why would I be okay? That's not even a question you should ask nobody in a situation like this... Am I okay? (Shuga) I can't believe you even brought her up here." Bree had stopped to turn to Shuga, then before Shuga could answer, proceeded to roast Kat. "Of course, I'm sure you just asked me that shit for something to say. It ain't like you care! You don't give a fuck about nobody but your-"

"Bree-" Shuga tried.

"Do not Bree me! You think it's supposed to be all good, like I'm happy to see you! Ohh, Kittie, you're out of prison... I! Don't! Give! A! Fuck! You knew what you were doing to get there. I just lost my baby and you coming up in here talking that dumb shit. 'Are you okay?' Yeah! Sure! Just peaches! My roses are red. My violets are blue. Why don't I just smoke some crack and be like you!"

"Bree!" Quent had heard enough and knew Bree well enough to know she was not gone stop. "She's just upset." Quent tried to apologize.

"Mineta, you hungry? Want to take her to the cafeteria?" Shuga asked Kat.

"Nope! I'm not hungry." But Mineta answered.

"Well, let's go get something to drink," Kat bought the hint for her to leave.

"Nope! I ain't thirsty either!" Mineta screamed back all in Bree's mouth, who had started back. She would be full of questions later.

Shuga grabbed Mineta's underarm pinching her, "I said go with your auntie to the cafeteria.

"Ouch! Shuga! You hurting my arm! Hell-" Mineta screamed but was pushed out the door with Kat.

"No! Fuck that! I don't wanna see her ass Fuck her! Hell!"

"I didn't know," Shuga cut in.

"Well, now, you do! I don't even understand why you got her living with you," Bree rolled her neck.

"She ain't got nowhere else to go." And that was the truth.

"So, it wouldn't be my problem. When all ya shit stole and sold!"

"Baby, calm down," Quent said, rubbing on his freshly cut head; two days ago, he had retired the dreads.

"What's up? Bree? Shuga?" Ross, Quent's boy, had walked in.

"Hey Ross," Shuga flirted.

***

Kat walked down to the cafeteria, wondering, would she ever be able to escape her past? Yeah, her choices had been bad, but shit, she had been young, really still a kid. Especially in her mind, if not body else, cause it was not like she ever had anyone to give her guidance. She hated that she had no one that she could turn to that without a doubt would be there for her, through the good, the bad, and the ugly. She stopped.

"Come on, auntie. Why is you just stopping and looking all crazy? Auntie Bree said you was crazy, but I don't know about believing her cause she talks bad about everybody, girl! Can't get along with nobody. I'm fo'real too! Come on now cause this ain't no Atlanta traffic," Mineta laughed, pulling Kat's hand.

Kat had stopped to take a breather from her thoughts. Those types of thoughts are what kept her turning back to the crack pipe. She could not fall back. She squeezed Mineta's little hand for strength that she did not know she was not given her, who was still going on and on talking about Bree and headed towards a vending machine.

"Kittie? Kittie! Kittie, bitch is that you? 'What?' Bitch, you done cleaned up! I thought that was yo' ass, but I wasn't fo' sho!" Joy walked up, spreading a non-joyful spirit. Joy was one of Kittie's old running buddies on occasion, back when Kittie was smoking. She did not run with her too hard cause Joy was known to be shiesty... But Kittie did run with Joy one time too many. Joy had hooked up with a big fat greasy muthafucker at a truck stop off of Fulton Industrial Boulevard... (FIB). Her m.o. from the go was to get his ass; he had said he wanted to hook up with a girl that would do it all. That was his fantasy. But not with Joy's facially challenged, unattractive man looking ass. She had remembered seeing Kittie walking back and forth earlier, and an idea popped instantly in her head, and she approached Kittie with the remixed version of the proposition.

Girl, this country ass nigga from Mississippi wanna spend something... but he want two girls." Joy knew Kittie was so out there that she would go along with anything for a buck. The trucker picked them up and was satisfied with Kittie. He paid Joy, then took them in his 18-wheeler to a rundown spot off of FIB. There they all got butt-naked and smoked crack. Then a knock came at the door. Joy ran to the door butt booty ass naked and stepped back as several of his friends came in the room. This was another part of the deal Kittie did not know about. But Kittie was so high she did not realize what was happening as the men took turns fucking her. All while Joy's stank ass watched sucking the pipe.

Kittie had not known what had went down but knew something was funny when she had pee'd out two condoms the next day. Later, word circled back to Kittie when Joy went around bragging on how she had pimped Kittie.

"Bitch! They said after you killed Turk that them people gave you life, and you wasn't never getting out of prison!" Joy yelled very loud and ghetto, disturbing the quietness of the hospital.

"You killed somebody?" Mineta jerked her neck around.

"No, baby," Kat answered. This is one thing Mineta didn't know why her auntie had went to prison but had asked a thousand times.

"I ain't see her. This yo' little girl? Who yo' daddy is? She look just like you," she told Kat as she waited on Mineta to answer her question- which was not gone happen. Mineta got the information, not give it away.

"No! This is Shuga's child."

"No, it ain't! She don't look nothing like no Shuga... Well, she said in disbelief, looking Kat up and down. She figured Kat had the baby during the time she was out there, and the little girl was blind to it all.

"Well, you got a few dollars you can hook a sister up with?" Kat dug in her pocket and gave Joy a five-dollar bill, thinking after all these years for her to still be on that shit, she sure had not lost no weight.

Joy then walked over to one of the vending machines, but not to buy nothing. She started kicking one of the machines screaming and hollering it ate her money, and ain't give her shit, causing a scene to get the attention of the cafeteria's staff. Kat remembered when she had use those same petty hustles, lying saying the machine took her money so she could get some change all for a hit.

"Who was that lady? What was she talking about? Mineta asked, just as nosey as ever. Never missing a beat.

"Nobody, Baby."

"Un-huh, she knew your name." Kat was saved from answering when Shuga walked in with Ross following.

"Kat! I came to give you some money. Can you take MARTA and get home with Mineta?"

"Wait a minute. MARTA? Are you serious?" Mineta started fussing. "Shuga, I don't wanna ride no bus. Why you can't just take us home? You brought us!"

"What I tell you about questioning grown folks?"

Mineta rolled her eyes.

"Yeah, I got her. And we don't need any money." Kat said, feeling funny and uncomfortable at being offered money by Shuga, who had once said she would never give Kat two quarters cause she knew what she would do with them... *Go get high.*

"Here. Take it anyway," she handed Kat a folded-up twenty-dollar bill, only a tiny portion of what she'd told Ross she needed to pay for a babysitter.

Chapter 4

That night Ross and Shuga started out at Club Hot Shot, where he had to oversee the night's events due to Quent's absence. Shuga walked in, and besides the dancer's, she was the only female up in the spot...

There was this group of dyke chicks, who were tipping more than the niggas, but to her, they did not count. Ross leads her to a private VIP area upstairs that had a balcony view that overlooked everything.

Tonight's featured stripper attention had been taken, and along with her attention being snatched, so were her dollars, when Shuga strutted up in the spot. Everyone assumed her to be a new girl, and with her ass so fat she was gone get shown love. So cheap ass niggas chose to put their dollars back in their pockets saving 'um to flex when the new girl hit the stage.

"She fine, ain't she?" Ross lame-ass came from behind her, whispering in her ear.

Shuga snapped her neck around to look at him, knowing if he thought the girl on stage was fine, she knew he thought of her as a goddess. Shuga ordered bottle after bottle of Grey Goose with Ross drinking it like water. By the time they left, Shuga had to help steady his intoxicated ass up.

"You want me to get him?" Paul, the club's bouncer, had asked, smiling goofy.

"N'all boo! We straight," Shuga smiled her million-watt smile back.

Paul was mesmerized watching Shuga's behind shift naturally from side to side as she led Ross to the passenger side door of his Navigator.

***

"Bitch, that nigga is gone already! Cuckoo for this Cocoa Puff," Kresa laughed lying. She was the one really gone cuckoo for his Cocoa Puff.

"Kresa, you talking bout skinny ass Eric, who used to be ballin' back in the day?" Shuga said, using emphasis on certain words. Her slick way of sending a message to Kresa that she had not got shit. Shuga did not like for folks to brag around her. She always had to be the one at all times showcasing.

"Shuga, I don't know what Eric you talking bout, but my Eric still the nigga to see, and yeah, he a little lean, but he right wit' it.

"Whatever, Kresa!" Shuga rudely changed the subject, not wanting to hear about what man Kresa had when she ain't have one herself! "I'm gone get this lion," she said, pointing out a lion with a king of the jungle type pose from the book of tattoos.

"Bitch, no!" Kresa jumped up, checking out all the pictures on the walls of the tattoo parlor. "I know this yo' first tat and all, but everyone got some type of cat, lion, or tiger on them, even if it's just the cat's claw. Bitch be original! Get a bear!"

"A bear? What the fuck? Bitch you trippin'!"

"I mean, shit'd lions, and tigers, and bears! Get some sugar bears... Shuga. Oohhh, look a starburst logo! Just like what Eric got airbrushed on his Monte' Carlo. I might get this threw on my right arm."

"There is no more room on your right arm, Kresa," Shuga said with distaste at all the tats. From Kresa's neck all the way down her right side ending at her baby toe, she was tatted up.

Shuga looked through the book and found two cub bears playing in honey. She decided to get those on her inner upper thigh.

***

Ross looked peaceful as he slept; all he was missing was a bed and a blanket. He was awaking by the buzzing of a fly, landing on his lips, trying its best to get in his stank shit smelling mouth. At the same spot since last night in Club Hot Shot's parking lot, with Shuga long gone and him butt naked and discombobulated.

Lost to all that had happened, he looked around stupefied, spotting a hump that appeared to be a body laying under the bus stop's bench that was to the side of the club.

As usual, it was old man Pete, a homeless white guy, who believed he was held back because he supported black and underneath the bench is where he made his home. What was not usual was Pete had Ross's clothes on.

"Yo', Pete! Yo', Pete!"

Pete leaned up, looking back. He did not appreciate being woke up while he was trying to sleep.

"Yo' nigga get yo' dirty as up out my clothes."

Pete looked down at his attire, then snapped up. "Nigga, fuck you! Go find ya own shit! Big baller! It's two dumpsters right over there," he giggled, showing those yuck yellow mushy soft-looking teeth, then laid back down on his don't know how many layers of clothes, without a worry in the world. He was not giving Ross shit nor thinking twice about his weak ass.

Ross had to end up driving home, butt naked to his momma house.

***

Smoke comes before the flames, and a person will always get the notice that destruction is headed their way if they stay focused and pay attention long enough to see the warning signs... then take heed. The first sign that something serious was in the making should have been seen when Bree made a big deal about her baby having a funeral.

A nurse had explained that most deceased fetuses and stillborn babies were donated to the School of Medicine over at Emory.

"Donate my baby? For some science experiment? Are you fucking crazy!" She screamed, snapping up so quick that the nurse had jumped and fumbled his clipboard, dropping it.

"Did you hear that?" She turned to Quent. "My flesh and blood. You want me to sign some fucking waiver, so y'all can cut my baby open and do whatever bullshit it is y'all wish to do with his precious little body? I don't fucking think so!"

"Ma'am, this is totally optional, and we cannot make you sign this. It was only a mere suggestion. Helping you only if you didn't want to go through the disposal of the body." His words were making things worst.

"I don't want to go through no fucking disposal, because I want my little baby hereeeeee-" She broke down in tears.

"I'm so sorry for your loss. I did not mean to upset you. I'll be leaving."

"Yeah, you get the fuck outta here," she screamed out behind her.

Later that evening, when she was released, she made Quent take her directly to Taylor and Sons' funeral home, where she picked out a powder blue casket that was the size of a man's shoe box. The next day would be the burial, and they would have a small memorial service.

Bree did not invite Shuga because she was still mad at her for bringing Kittie to her hospital room. She did not want anything to do with that woman, and she did not want that woman knowing anything about her and... Quent.

Bree remembered all the stories about Kittie and her willingness to fuck anything around her for a few bucks...

Sometimes only one dollar, all to go feed her dope habit. And Bree knew that Kittie had not completely recovered. That Kittie was still a crackhead, and like that white girl Lindsay L., she was just waiting for a comeback. Bree could bet that Kittie's habit was just on hiatus. The only reason why she looked halfway decent was because the prison did not offer crack, and that was the only reason why she was not using the drug. Not because she did not want to, but the lack of availability gave her no choice but to quit.

Those were her reasons!

Quent thought she hated her sister for that, but it seemed a little deeper than that. All while growing up, Kittie had been like the momma to Bree, filling her head up with all kinds of dreams. Dreams that later went up in smoke when she hit the crackpipe. Kittie was the one that gave Bree that small slither of hope that life could be better then what they were living. She was also the same one who snatched it away when she left to pursue her career at being a crackhead hoe.

Bree was then lost, her dreams vanished, her thoughts faded. There was no better life out there.

Shuga had always been about self, so that was her norm.

But Kittie- Kittie had been her inspiration.

Then Kittie broke her heart, becoming what she preached to Bree about not being.

Only Bree was different. Always seriously focused. She always knew she was the strong one. She vowed not to become a statistic.   She was gone do better with her life... And she had. Everything would have been perfect if...

It's like the simple mention of Kittie's name had done nothing but bring on a domino effect of bad luck. Ever since Shuga first told her that Kittie was coming home, nothing good had happened...

Now, as she sat draped in all black, she cried and cried wishing things could go back one week. Just one week! Then Quent tried to comfort her by telling her that they would have more babies. Only that was not helping her. It was not that easy. And she wished he would stop saying that shit! Cause even if they could, this one could not be replaced. But the truth was they would never have a child together.

And he wanted a child. She needed a baby but would never be able to have one naturally.

Bree stood in the funeral parlor long after everybody had left, snapping shot after shot of little Quentin Jr.

She swore he had smiled at her, then as she was about to leave, her baby told her he was scared and did not want to be by himself and asked her to stay a little longer... She stayed the whole night.

***

Kresa was not even all the way out of the tattoo parlor when she started back up on her man. Shuga quickly burst her bubble, having an *'aha moment'* of recollection, and remembering exactly who Eric was. Not only who he was, but who he was wife'n these days.

"Bitch I am so telling you! Nigga is on seriously! And he was all up on who? Me! That's right! The whole night! So, I could care less about all that other fuck shit. I don't give two fucks about Erica or how crazy they say she is. She ain't never crossed my path... Cause if she does ba-by! *Shit gone be poppin'*!" Kresa sung out the last part on beat with the Chris Brown song.

Shuga frowned at her so-called best friend, Kresa. "But why would yo' ass wanna go through all that drama?"

"Why? Bitch, what you mean, why?"

"Bitch, don't play, you know exactly what the hell I mean! Eric ain't shit. And here yo' ass is sittin' up there getting all serious, wanting to fall in love." *"Like the simple bitch you are,"* Shuga said to herself. "Him and Erica have been rocking. He cheats on her ass, fucking any and all that'll let him, but he not gone leave her." *Another hit!* "It ain't never happened." *Stupid!* "What, you think you the one that's gone make a change? Aight, *'man in the mirror,'*" Shuga laughed, remembering so much about Eric all of a sudden.

"Kresa, them people been together so long, they look like brother and sister. Hell, they even got names that sound alike...And with all them kids. Bitch, where you gone fit in at? They got too much going on!"

"Bitch, I ain't tryin to fit in with none of that. I'm simply going to take him away from all that. Watch me now! He tired of her ass and is too thirsty for me. He just needed the right woman. And he found her. You heard me? He wants to wife me! But only two things I want from him right now, his big black dick and his long green dollars. I been getting both, and I'ma keep getting both." As usual, Kresa extended the truth. One of those qualities she was lying about and could not possibly be getting because one of those qualities Eric did not possess. But for now, she had front.

"Aight, I'm just saying! When shit blow up..." Shuga smirked. She was always one to know best and always one to give advice, but let that same advice play on deaf ears when it came to her.

Kresa turned quickly, letting out a loud chest heaving huff. "See! That's why the fuck I don't tell yo' ass shit. Why you always gotta be actin' like somebody momma and shit."

"Whatever!" Shuga snapped.

Evil-eyed, Kresa thought, *"You fucking jealous bitch! If yo' ass woulda met him first, you wouldn't be talking this shit. Hating ass can't never be happy for nobody. For once, I got a good nigga in my life, and you just mad."* Kresa ended her thoughts with a smile of malice.

Silence...

More silence...

Long silence...

None of which Shuga liked. When a person was quiet, it gave them a chance to think, something she did not like for folks to do while in her presence. She would hate for a person to see through her and her conniving ways. She had to stay on top and not let nobody get one up on her. She was one to always try to manipulate every situation so that when the results came in, they would flow her way. Breaking the unwanted silence, she looked over and said, "Do whatever you gotta do. You know you is my girl! What the fuck? I ain't gone have my girls back? I'm ridin' wit cha Boo! Let Erica bring it. I'll run her ass over." She lied; what she really meant was she would run the other way with her scary ass.

Kresa did not buy that fake ass shit for two seconds. Already knowing what was up with Shuga and Redman, *not a damn thing*, but being messy, Kresa asked about him anyway. "So, what's up with you and that nigga Redman that you hooked up with at the Lucky Lounge?" Let Kresa rain a little.

"Shit," she mumbled too quickly, then wondered if it showed just what she was trying to hide. She would never reveal that she went out like a nickel and dime hoe, by fucking and sucking after only a couple hours of knowing him and without getting shit upfront.

Shuga did not get nothing, not even an after-breakfast meal to re-energize from all that fucking, they had done. She straight played herself. She knew better. Shuga had done that same shit that she was always talking about other simple hoes for doing. And she knew Redman was balling! And she had thought she had her game on point and that Redman would be whipped and wife her. Wrong! That was a dun-da-ta!

Too bad for Shuga, cause he had liked her fo'real. Had been sweating her, until her hoe tactics showed.

"Damn," Shuga unconsciously said under her breath.

Kresa catching her disappointment, looked over and asked, "Huh?"

"Oh, nothing. Bitch, I left that heat on. Damn, you know that shit'll run my bill straight up." She lied.

"Oh," Kresa said, then started singing along with Jay-Z and crew on 'Run This Town' remixing the words she did not know which were most of them. "Life's a game, but it's not fair. I break the rules cause I don't care. I walk so tall and look for victory! A-a-a-ahh-ahh." Then suddenly, she started screaming, acting straight retarded. "Oh shit! Oh shit! Did you just hear that? Ahhhaaa! Oh, my God! Oh, my God! Oh, my God!" She screamed, jumping to turn V103 up louder. "Da Snowman is gone be at the Chameleon Club tonight!" She screamed again louder, kicking around in the seat while fanning herself. Shuga couldn't stand when Kresa dumb ass acted like a fucking groupie. "Come on bitch! Hit 85! We gots to head out to the Lenox, so we can get fresh on they ass. And yes, I got a fresh one!" She screamed again, producing a platinum Visa card.

"Ching-ching" rang in Shuga's ear as she cut lanes hitting the I-85 ramp easily.

They made it to the Lenox Square mall without the usual rush hour stop and go Atlanta traffic, but had to bum rush an old white couple out of a parking space that they had patiently waited on. Neither cared, though. Shuga got her car in first, and that was that.

"Damn, girl!" Kresa patted her head. "How does my hair look?" She asked Shuga.

"The same as it did this morning," Shuga barked out, tooting her nose up behind Kresa's back while thinking, 'A mess!' Then mumbled. "Only you would rock it."

"Huh?"

"I said you is rocking it!"

"It" was a multicolored green, pink, blue, and purple mini spikes at the top with longer weave flips down the back, all together forming a mohawk. Truth be told, Shuga was just hating. Always, whenever somebody did something, she could not, and she knew she would never have the nerve to pull anything quite that unique off. Yet, on Kresa with all her piercings and tats, it actually fit her, gave her a grungy runway model look.

The two strutted up in the Lenox with their head held as if they had a million bucks just to spend there, and it would not dent their pockets an inch.

Inside of Sak's Fifth Avenue, Shuga's eyes caught a Giambattista white leather halter top with a white Valentino pony hair mini skirt to pair together. She snatched it up. Only a bad bitch could pull off white in the wintertime, and she was just that bad bitch to do it.

But since it was one of those true winter days that was really cold, she would need a coat. She spotted a white leather chinchilla fur-trimmed trench that she would wear over her itty-bitty outfit, only until she got in the club.

Saks Fifth was making it hard for a bitch in choosing, with their shoe game so on point. Shuga could not decide if she wanted the white leather thigh high heel and toe freeboots or the clear six-inch strap up stilettos, both by Tom Ford and both with price tags over two thousand dollars. "What the hell! You only live once!" She got both and would make a choice later on which she would wear.

Secretly, Shuga and Kresa were in competition with each other, since they both knew that ballers would be in place, like roaches in the projects. Neither one ever stopped to think that there would be enough paid men for both to go around without always trying to outdo the other. They did not think like that, though. Shuga always wanted all of the men with deep pockets to be up on her, and so did Kresa, who only just recently adopted that trait. But Kresa was a follower to her so-called bestie. So, of course, she had to go all out and be seen too.

Kresa looked for something that would complement her proudest asset. Which was her blow-up booty. She found a diamond-studded black Dolce & Gabbana bra with jeans from 7 for all Mankind, that was so skintight that they looked like they had been spray-painted on. Her outfit was right, plus it would put all of her tats on display. For her feet, she grabbed up a pair of Balenciaga, and it just so happen that they were the highest open toe stiletto heels in the department. Then a little red Bally leather military type jacket, and just for some personalized flavor, she copped a two-thousand-dollar leather collar by Sergio Rossi, and now her ensemble was complete.

The stolen credit card would be burnt out by tomorrow morning, as they walked out with almost twenty thousand dollars on just a couple of one-time wear outfits. But when does it matter how much you spend when the money's not yours?

"Bitch you know we gots to ride in style!" Kresa said, jumping around once they were back in Shuga's car.

"What the fuck you mean style?" Shuga flared her nose, asking straight offended. "Bitch you ain't even got no car!" Shuga turned to look at her in disbelief. *"Trick! Better yet, yo' ass is twenty-four and can't even drive. I don't even know why I fool up with yo' simple scrub ass,"* Shuga thought, then relaxed remembering exactly why: All the free clothes Kresa had gotten for her over the years, just as a return of giving her free rides to the malls to use hot credit cards or bad checks. That is why the fuck she fooled with the shiesty bitch.

"N'all girl. Nothing like that. Your Charger straight-" Kresa said, getting interrupted.

"Bitch you ain't gotta tell me what I know! Cause I know, it is! It's a what? Two thousand ten! And this is what? Two thousand nine? Yeah, that's what's up! Gotta be! And oh, I work where? Nowhere! Ha! Yeah, that's what's up!" Shuga nodded her head, checking Kresa with every word. "And you got a what?" She looked over and smirked.

"See bitch! You had to go there! And that ain't even what the fuck I meant. Cause if I could drive, I'd have me something that was ole school. All I was saying is you already know it ain't gone be nothing but big trucks with even bigger rims, futuristic foreign cars, and supped up ole schools designed all up. We need something flashy too! That is all. And since it's too late to order you some rim, let's do the next best thing."

Shuga rolled her eyes, still offended, feeling like Kresa was just trying to sugarcoat and kiss ass. "And what would that be?" She spit out.

"Let's call and reserve a muthafuckin' red big boy Hummer-"

"A stretch Hummer? Oh... Okay," Shuga was all smiles, going along with it now, as she envisioned how she would look stepping out at the same time, picturing the unit on Redman's face when she would stunt on his ass.

Redman was destined to be somewhere hot and popping in the A, trying to be seen. And the hot and popping spots were the only places they had share their time with.

Tonight, it would be on!

***

Kresa made reservations for the stretch Hummer giving the limo service the platinum visa card number, with instructions for them to be picked up at the 'W' hotel on Piedmont at eight o'clock sharp.

The plan was for them to go to the 'W' acting as if they were registered guests, hanging out in the lobby waiting for their driver to arrive. Once they got back, they would again enter the hotel as guests being dropped off, but when the coast was clear, they'd bailout through the back door to the parking garage where Shuga's Charger would be waiting.

The plan was set. It was six forty-five, so they each had over an hour to do their thing... Well, Kresa did because after Shuga dropped her off at home, she still had to turn right back around and pick her up. Good thing for Shuga was her hair and nails were already done. Stayed done! Hair game and nail game stayed on point.

Kresa hated that original wrap style that Shuga kept in her head, forever combing one side over, so it swooped and hung in her eye like the late singer Aaliyah had signature. But even she had stopped sporting that hairstyle and upgraded long before she passed.

Ole girl was stuck in a nineties time warp. Little did Shuga know. But you could not tell her that, and with them ultra-long whore red nails, she sported them shits played out in the eighties.

As Shuga drove Kresa home, Kresa just stared at her. One plus for Shuga was her hair, old fashioned as it was, it was long and thick... if it was all hers. Come to think about it, Kresa did not know if it was all hers or not.

Hating, Kresa assumed it probably was a weave, maybe some infusions, cause the shit was never outta place.

Shuga skidded to a stop, and Kresa jumped out of the car, running to her house, undressing as she rushed to the bathroom. Right as she was about to get in the shower, she decided she could not take one. The shower's steam would mess up her hair, causing her hard spikes to melt and fall... So, she said to herself. Unadmitted, the girl just didn't like water, so she took a wet rag, unsoaped and wiped at her musty underarms that had been sweating all day, her twangy pocketbook that was equally wet from the heat of excitement, then on to her butty hole. She smelled the rag, which was funky to death, then threw it. She splattered on a half-bottle of Curve lotion in attempts to cover any leftover unnatural smells. Next came the new outfit. Checking herself out, she looked in her full-length mirror and noticed that her underarms had gray-brown clumps of balled up deodorant knots. She picked at each of the balls until they were gone. She should shave her hairy armpits then thought fuck it, was not enough time. Heavily, she sprayed herself down in the Curve perfume that matched the lotion. She thickly applied too much Mac eyeshadow in bright out of season colors... and with that hair! Then, she swiped on globs of mascara over her already heavily coated mascara'd eyes and knew she could not be touched.

All she had to do now was wait for Shuga to scoop her back up. She did that as she watched an episode of one real, plus one phony, and three desperate Housewives of Atlanta, smoking a blunt.

***

Shuga had gotten home rushing as well. She wrapped her head in a silk scarf and threw a shower cap over it as she jumped in the shower. Quickly doing everything, she was back at Kresa' s house within the hour, not only looking but feeling like a few million bucks. No one could tell her that she was not the baddest bitch.

Anxious, she could not wait to see Redman's ass. In fact, she wanted only to go all the places she knew he would be, but did not want to be oblivious with her stalking. She just wished he would be there when she stepped out that Hummer, so he could think about how he played her, and he wished he had not. She wanted him to say something to her so she could dis his ass for that bullshit he pulled. She could imagine his face souring.

Shuga knew when niggas saw her looking this rich, they all would be drooling with lust. This she could envision as they jumped in the back of the Hummer, too excited to wait on the driver to open the door and help them in the big ass truck. The driver walked to the back, trying to be professional but coming off just as ghetto as the projects on check day.

"Ma'am's are you with Dr. A-la-bema party?" The way the driver questioned them was like they had just jumped up in his shit for a free ride for the hell of it.

"Dr. Alabera," Kresa corrected him, catching an attitude. He will not be getting not a dime in tips for that little stunt he pulled.

"Yes ma'am, yes ma'am," he nodded to both of them, just like the house nigga as he shut the door. Once he was back up front, he slided the dark window separating them down, turning looking like a cartoon, he asked. "Where to?"

"Lame ass!" Kresa thought, but said, "We heard on the radio earlier, something about the rapper Da Snowman being at a club tonight?" She tried to act like an out of towner, what the neurosurgeon, Dr. Alabera, really would be instead of the Grady baby she really was.

"Yeah, yeah, he gone be at the Chameleon Club," the driver said, getting amped up.

"Well, do you know where this Chameleon Club is located?"

"Of course, of course," he snickered.

"That is where we want to go then, but its only eight. So, we don't want to get there, until say elevenish... Drive us to the-" she caught herself. "Just take us by all the happening spots, alright?" Kresa ordered as she slide the tinted window back up. She then raided the minibar.

"Bitch, they gots Mo', Remy and oh shit Henn-doggy-dog," she said, grabbing all the bottles, tossing Shuga a bottle of Remy VSOP and a blunt. "Light this!"

Shuga knew this would be her night. She could feel it in the air.

Kresa had opened the moon roof and was hanging out dancing. "Bitch get yo' ass up here and check this shit out," she screamed, yanking on Shuga's arm with her ass bobbing all in Shuga's face.

Shuga's nose caught a whiff of funk, and it was not from the skunk they had just blazed. Well damn, she hoped Kresa had bathed while trying to floss in them expensive ass clothes. Sometimes, Shuga just could not believe Kresa. She pulled herself up through the moon roof and felt like Miss America leading the parade as everybody waved, whistled, and yelled out, asking could they ride.

Shuga was feeling herself. Something about being in the city of Atlanta that caused extreme excitement, just in the vibrant atmosphere. Cruising down the brightly lit streets just went to a person's soul and motivated excitement, optimism, and inspiration.

The night's air had turned cold, and even wrapped up in the fur leather trench, Shuga was freezing. But she did only have that mini halter getup on underneath it. But since she rocked it like it was designed especially for her voluptuous body, she did not think about the weather. She looked better than good, and that was all that mattered!

After, awhile Kresa brought her funky ass in; her voice was all hoarse, and her hair was wind blow each and every way. Kresa could not wait to be at the club, since she knew I'm it posted would be nothing but the ballers from the A and out of town niggas that were getting it in. She also knew Eric's ass would be there, but she did not want him sweating her like that, not tonight. Cause this night, she had a few tricks up her sleeve. Actually, this night she planned to get Da Snowman's dick. She just was not about to share that idea with no one, especially not Shuga's ass. She knew she would hate, and not only hate but would probably want him for herself. So, this was one plan that was plotted out in her head solo and would stay. She fired up another Swisher Sweet filled with skunk and laid-back grooving with Plies, 'I got plenty money,' all while scheming.

Chapter 5

Part of Kat's release was an order to go meet with a probation officer within seventy-two hours. Prior to her prison bid, she had gotten caught up with a bad check charge and had gotten a year on paper. So, for the next twelve months, she would have to put up with this month after month bullshit and keep herself straight.

Her parole officer, who seemed pretty cool at first, gave her a list of places that would possibly hire convicted felons and advised her to check them out. Then he hit her with a hard one because she had a history of drug abuse, P.O. dude gave her the business, warning her that she would be subject at random to drug screenings... Then he popped a cup down in front of her, losing any and all cool points he had with her. She now remembered the reason why she did not like people who worked for any type of law enforcement period. She was glad now that her willpower had not failed and caused her to give in to that leftover blunt that was in Shuga's ashtray. She did not even know how she had allowed herself to look at it twice.

Kat left the probation office a nervous wreck, jumping every time someone shouted or a loud noise was made. Shell-shocked from her dehumanizing prison experience. She walked to the Marta train station dressed in Shuga's pink and gray BCBG velour jogging suit with matching pink and gray Air Force Ones. She grabbed everyone's attention as all eyes were on her ridiculously dumb booty. It synchronized a pattern from left to right. She did not know that, though. Paranoia had her thinking that everybody was looking at her cause they knew she had just got out of prison and had to wear her sister's tight-fitting clothes. She got in line, standing next to a chick that looked to be about her age.

"Ohh," the girl squeaked in horror and had Kat wondering if she was someone from her past, until she asked, "Where you get yo' nails did at?"

"Huh?" Kat answered, dumbfounded, clearly not understanding, because she had not once in her life had her nails done by anybody other than Shuga when they used to play dress up as kids.

"Who be doing yo' nails?" the girl waited on Kat to answer, but she was still confused at the question. The chick, then, broke it down. "You need to let me know, so I can make sure I don't go there. That shit looks nasty, and I'll spread the word, cause I got a blog," she pointed a neatly French manicured false nail at Kat's gnawed off middle finger. "That fungus look real bad! I'd sue they ass if I was you. Get you a lawyer and go to the doctor too, cause that shit'll spread. You know them ching-chong muthafuckas don't know what they be doing when it comes to sanitation. You got a card handy from them?"

Kat slumped and walked off from the chick, who was dead ass seriously waiting for an answer. She would just walk back to Shuga's cause she needed to air her head...

Realizing where she was at, her walk would be like ten miles, so she decided to just walk three blocks over to the bus line. Her feelings were hurt. The ugly fingernail was a leftover souvenir, reminding her of what she was and where she had been. A memory she could never escape. She would never be able to hide or outrun her past...so why try to? Somebody was always remembering something about her past, then bringing it up. Each time it caused her to rehash pain-filled memories. Of the truth! And each time, it caused a cloud of depression to overshadow her.

With depression always came those thoughts... thoughts of just how worthless she had been and felt, since those days back after their mom left. But with those thoughts always came an answer for relief. The only time relief was present was when she was high. She knew it tried to fight it, but still in the back of her head, a little voice could be heard, whispering, letting her know to never forget that there was a cure. There was a false ray of hope just calling and waiting on her to make the first move, and from there, he could take over. An answer to all problems.

When she had those thoughts in prison, it was different because she could not act out on them; therefore, she could fight it without even trying. But now came the real test. She was free and once again had access to it all.

Questions surfaced. Could she fight it? Was Kat strong enough?

She had not been out, but three days and here she was already thinking about it. She flared her nose in frustration, shaking the thoughts away, she rolled her eyes as she noticed a shabby sign that read check cashing. She walked around the corner and stepped inside the place.

"You can't be serious. You mean to tell me you gonna charge me six dollars and thirty cents to cash a measly ass thirty-five-dollar check? This some bullshit."

"Yes. That tis correct now don't cuss me," the Arabic man seated behind a bulletproof window stated plainly, then pointed to a sign which advertised charges: 10% with valid I.D. and 18% without valid I.D.

"But, I do have an I.D."

"It tis, not a *valid* I.D."

"Yes, it tis! It's issued by the state of Georgia."

"No! It is not. It tis given out by Georgia prison. Prison I.D., not valid I.D. Prison I.D. show you commit crime." He said, then fixed his turban, which was about to fall from his exaggerated head movements. He stood from the stool. "You want to cash or not?"

"Sure, what the hell! Why not?"

"You no get smart with me. I help you!"

Kat cashed the check, then walked out and spotted several shops down the street that were not there prior to her prison bid. One of which was an Asian nail salon. She stepped inside and asked a woman who did not have anyone at her station could she do a whole nail coverup to camouflage one of her nails. The woman turned and called what seemed to be every Asian in the joint. Some even left their customers. Kat got embarrassed as everyone looked her way, trying to see what all the commotion was about. Her cheeks grew hot as she knew the whole place talked about her.

Finally, a man broke off from the little huddle who spoke English. "Who do yo' nails?"

Why does everyone keep asking that dumb ass question?

"No one," she answered softly.

"Where the fungus come from?" He said loud and very clear. Muthafucka ain't never spoke English that good. Kat turned to see if any of the black customers had heard.

They had!

And they were watching.

"It's not a fungus. I was bitten here," she pointed.

"Ooohhh," they all said at the same time with the same blank expression on their faces, then went back to talking their language.

After a while, they dispersed, and one pulled her by her good hand and over to a station. The girl began working filing hard on the nail that grew into a ragged hump, into a smooth little odd-shaped nail. Half an hour later, the girl was done, and Kat had what looked like a new set of hands. Her confidence level grew as she walked out of the nail salon admiring the work.

Eyes bright, she could not help but smile. Even though it had cost almost forty dollars, it was worth it. She was now nearly broke. Having gotten an envelope that first day she had got out from Shuga that she supposedly had saved from people who were looking out that contained fifty dollars now, but originally way more, and that twenty for babysitting.

Kat pulled out that job list and looked through it. She was going to have to get one as soon as possible. While standing at the corner waiting to cross the street, a car suddenly braked loud and hard, causing the car behind it to run slap into the back of it.

They were both two big old clunky models, so they did not just fold up like new cars would have. They kind of just stuck to each other.

"Damn!" The driver of the first vehicle just sat staring. Kat hadn't even realized she was what had caused the fender bender as she walked around them.

"Shawty! Aye-aye! Shawty! Aye-aye! Shawty, what's up with cha?"

Kat turned, as the driver had jumped out and was approaching her. "What's up with me? You need to be worried about them folk's car!" She said.

"N'all they need to be worried bout mine, that shit hit me," he said, pointing back at the old Buick, right as his phone rung. He glanced down but did not take the call. "My paint job cost more than that whole car worth." He smiled cutely, revealing a mouthful of gold and diamond teeth.

"Ohh, I remember you. You is Monty's lil' brother, Lemonhead."

"Yeah, but don't nobody call me that no mo... Baby girl, that's been gone. They call me LA."

"LA? I bet yo' Granny, Ms. Pearl, still calling you Lemonhead."

"So shawty, you know a nigga whole fam?"

"Something like that, well, you should know a nigga straight," he said as his phone rang again. He one second glanced it.

"Umph... Aye, look," Kat was thrown off as she pointed to dude in the hooptie. He had crept out, unhooked his bumper from LA's Chevy Impala, and was slowly backing the Buick out. As soon as he got clearance, he burnt rubber. LA had to jerk Kat from just standing in the street, or dude who looked to be a straight-up fiend with that crazed drugged outlook would have at least bumped a hip. They were right up on each other and could not help but laugh when they saw the hysterical expression on his face.

Kat jumped, moving shyly out of LA's grip.

"That car probably stolen."

"Ya think?"

LA shrugged his shoulders. "Hold up shawty. Let me pull out da street before 5.0 pull up," he told her.

"Okay. Well, I gotta catch the bus anyway," Kat said, waving bye. She turned, just as he grabbed her tiny waist from behind. He pulled her back to his driver's side door, then pushed her inside the car. "Aye, what the hell wrong with you? Didn't Ms. Pearl teach you better than that? Boy, you gots to respect your elders!"

"Elders?" LA laughed.

"Boy. I'm old enough to be your momma," Kat said, attempting to put one up on him.

"Girl get outta here," he said, as she held her serious face. "For real?"

"Yes!" She nodded.

"How old are you?"

"Forty-two," she said, trying her best to keep from laughing.

"Forty-two? Damn! You look good! I thought you was bout, say twenty-eight... twenty-nine."

"Twenty-eight or twenty-nine?" She screamed at him offensively. "I know I don't look that damn old. I was just playing with yo' ass. But I am a lot older than you. Twenty-six."

"Well, I'm twenty-four, so you not much older than me."

Kat thought something did not seem right. She seemed to remember LA being a little boy tagging along behind his brother, when she was out there, but then, she was forgetting that she had took to the streets at the age of twelve. Her thoughts were interrupted by the ringing of his phone again. "You might wanna get that."

"N'all I'm straight." Again, he did not take the call.

"How you knew, Monty?"

"Just from round da way. He good?"

"So, you didn't know he passed?" LA said unemotionally.

"No, I didn't. I'm sorry to hear that."

"Yeah. A accident. We put him away good. At his memorial, the whole city came out. We did it big! Police came shut down his homecoming. Where you been? Everybody came out."

Kat got quiet, not ready to tell him of her prison experience. "Boy, you don't wanna know. Where in the hell is you taking me?" She changed the subject.

"I was on my way to make a run."

"A run? Nigga if you don't pull this car over. I'm on probation, and you trying to get me caught up."

"Never that. So, I got me a thug girl? What you do?"

"Murder."

"You on probation for murder? Yeah, um-huh, you should be a comedian," he said, turning down English Ave. This was a part of the city known as the Bluff, notorious for drug dealing and Kittie's old stomping grounds.

"Oh, no, the probation is for a check charge. Nigga, I know you ain't bring me in no damn Bluff. Oh, hell, no! Get me the hell outta here," she said, ducking down in her seat.

"What is you doing all that for?" He laughed, but she was dead ass serious.

"Those bullets they be spraying ain't got no name on them."

"What? You been watching too much news." And she had! In prison, all the inmates wanted to watch was news or Lifetime, like they could not look around for both. "Don't believe that bullshit. Besides you riding with a soldier, that'll stand up for ya. I got you!"

"Whatever!" She said, continuing to stay as far down in her seat as she could. He pulled up in front of a house on Neal St.

"Come on."

"I ain't going in there."

"N'all we straight. This my auntie's house."

"I'll sit right here," she said, looking over at the house that did look like somebody's aunties. It was well kept, considering its surroundings. He jumped out, accidentally leaving his phone on the seat. It rang, and she quickly glanced over at it, as he was headed back to the car with a small duffle bag in his hand.

"Your phone rang again. A picture came up. Was that Khloe Kardashian?"

"No!" He got nervous.

"She must be a lookalike then." He did not respond. "Listen, I am not about to be riding around all these different dope neighborhoods with you! You know how 5.0 be racial profiling us, black folks. Plus, you in dis pimped-out Chevy. This looks like a dope boy car. So, hell n'all drop me off at the nearest MARTA station, and I can make it from there. And it looks like your girl looking for you. You may want to make yourself available," she added and didn't know why. She had only known him for what ten-fifteen minutes? And besides, if he really knew who he had picked up, he would be pushing her ass out.

"Shawty, stop tripping. I got you, and I ain't got no girl. Shawty, you is my thug girl, so chill," he told her as they crossed over Joseph E. Lowery and pulled up to a yellow house. He picked up his phone. "I'm out here," Then turned the phone's power off. He jumped out as a little girl, no more than twelve came out. They exchanged bags, and Kat knew the streets were getting worse every day.

Kat watched and took it all in. LA had an air of power to him and was fine. She knew he had money, and, for one day, she wish she could be like her sister, Shuga, if only for a day. Shuga knew how to rack a baller up, and LA was doing just that. If Shuga would have had this opportunity, she would have had this nigga nose wide open and her pockets full. But Kat did not know what to do or say. Nor did she feel confident enough to even be with a nigga of his status. She was a recovering crack head convict hooker. She knew LA would not want her for real.

Could not possibly... *Maybe to fuck.*

So, what the hell, and if he did, maybe she would fuck him. She had not had none in over five years. Just thinking about it had her flushed.

"Shawty, what the hell you smiling so hard for? Me?" He had snuck up on her while she was in thought.

"No! No reason! Why the hell you ain't started this car?" She asked, looking around. She decided she would make the best of this opportunity. It only knocks once.

As soon as they were out of the Bluff, she leaned over and kissed him. He was shocked. "What you gotta do?"

"I ain't got shit to do. I'm chilling. You, the man. What you gotta do?"

"Just be with you," he said, getting on the 285 headed to his spot in College Park. A suburban city just south of Atlanta.

"This where you live?" Kat could not believe it when they pulled into a three-car garage with sixteen feet ceilings. He jumped out, rushing to her door.

She saw a Benz and what looked like a Porsche truck. 'Did they even make those?' She wondered, then knew for a fact that LA was up there with this dope ass crib and those fat ass rides it showed without question just how much.

Quickly, her confidence level diminished. "There is no way he gone want the real me," Kat silently said as she was led through a side door that took them to his kitchen. She was purely amazed, never seeing the inside of a house this plush. He led her down five steps that opened up to a huge sunken den. He flipped on the lights and handed her a remote.

"Chill, I'll be right back."

Glancing around, Kat walked over to his bar. It was filled with all sorts of liquor. She chose a peach Alize and gulped it down while she sat down and flipped through channels. She settled on a music video channel. She needed to catch up on the latest music. Prison did not have cable, so everything would be new. LA ran down the steps, scaring her, as he jumped over the back of the couch, flopping down next to her.

"What's up?"

"You," she replied, feeling lifted from the drink.

LA leaned up and flipped a drawer down off the coffee table and came back up with a Backwood and a tray of weed. "Roll me up."

"I can't smoke!" She said, getting upset at the temptation. If only he knew of the strong addiction, she battled, and it all started with what she was looking at now. So, it was not really all about her parole, but for now, she would use that. "I just got a drug test today! I told yo' ass I am on probation. What? You thought I was playing? "

"Shawty... Okay. Thug girl," he interlocked his hand inside hers. "Damn you just as yellow as me."

"I ain't never had-" They said in unison. Neither had ever been with anyone more than two shades short of a Hersey bar. They laughed, realizing they were thinking the same thing.

LA rolled his blunt and puffed about two times, then put it out. He leaned into her, looking chinky-eyed.

"What's up?"

"I told you. You," she leaned in to kiss his forehead, only he caught her lips with his. She opened her mouth as he pushed his tongue inside, making her wet.

LA cupped her round braless breast through the jacket, then unzipped it. He eased her out of it and started sucking on her pink nipples, which were rock hard. His cool nibbling quenched the hot ache that had developed inside of them. He stood up, pulling her with him. He slid her out of her bottoms and just stared at her perfect smooth body.

"Damn, you is fine!"

"Stop staring," she pushed his face in embarrassment.

"I mean damn. You got a nigga drooling. Turn around."

"No," she said, feeling ashamed, never liking to be given compliments, because of the issues still buried deep inside of her.

"Why? You is beautiful. You got ass and hips without all the stretch marks."

"I don't have kids," she blurted.

Her body was truly a blessing from what he was used to seeing... Hood girls came with million dollar faces but food stamp bodies or vice versa. It was rare to find one with both. But here he had he was going to keep this one around.

He grabbed her juicy ass with both hands, squeezing, pulling her towards his face. He muzzled his face around in her pussy.

Never, when LA fucked a girl for the first time, would he eat them out, but with Kat, lust had him wanting to satisfy her in every way he could. He slid her thong down and propped one of her tight thighs up on his shoulder and went at her licking. Eyes closed; they were both in heaven. He felt as her clitoris grew hard, but he did not stop. He kept licking until she skeeted on his face. Quickly her drunk all her juices. Kat was in ecstasy. LA pulled his pants down then sat back; arms folded behind his head. She straddled him, as his head touched the opening of her hot wet vagina, heat passed through her entire soul, then he hip thrust himself inside of her. As he shoved, he himself more, she screamed out in pain and pleasure.

"Aye, Shawty, are you a virgin?"

"What? Nigga no!"

"Damn, it's so tight and wet," he moaned, pushing more of his ten inches inside of her. She moaned loud but was determined to keep up with him. He held onto her hips as he gyrated around in her warmth. The moment crept upon him when he could not hold out any longer, one more stroke, and he shot off like a Mossberg. A full load pumped inside of her.

Then and only then did he remember what a condom was.

Chapter 6

Making its presence known, the cherry red stretch Hummer pulled up in front of the Chameleon Club, demanding boldly that everyone stop whatever it was they were doing to notice it, as it stunted without even trying.

Just as Shuga had figured, Redman was on the scene posted directly across the street from the club with a flock of low rate bum bitches, surrounding him like he was the star that people had dressed their best for.

Anxious, Kresa grabbed the handle of the door, ready to jump out and get it started, but Shuga snatched her back. "Wait on, dude, to open the door! Bitch tonight. We is gone have some class!" She said while thinking that Kresa was so tacky.

"Oh-yeah-yeah! Right bitch!" She said, swaying her body and fingering that hair again.

The driver walked to the back, looking just as goofy as he really was, and opened the door, and Kresa leaped out smiling uncontrollably, and it's like everyone around the club had paused to stare. She stopped to pose, loving the attention as she stood in her giving it to the haters' stance while waiting on Shuga, who was exiting gracefully. Shuga eased out, allowing her leather and fur trench coat to fly backward like a cape, creating an illusion of pure glamour.

"Who is that?"

"Y'all, y'all look!"

"Who they is?"

They heard people from the crowd asked.

"Is they with Da Snowman?"

"You know they is!"

"Is that...."

"Yeah - yeah - y'all, that's her!"

"That's that rapper chick from Miami!"

Shuga heard another group say and knew they were talking about her and her resemblance to the self-proclaimed baddest bitch in the rap game, Trina. Shuga turned slightly to make sure Redman, who had eyes their way had his eyes her way. Shuga read his lips as his mouth formed her name questioning. She watched him dust his hands down on his pants, a stupid habit she noticed he done a lot as he walked away from the group of crumb bums to head across the street towards her.

Like it was that easy.

Shuga continued with her star-studded role, acting as if she could see no one, including him. They were at the door, ignoring the long ass line like they had it like that, knowing they were not on nobody's VIP list.

"Yo' Shuga, let me holla at cha for a minute."

"Excuse me?" She said, snapping her neck around like this ain't exactly what she wanted.

"Yo'! Let me holla at cha!" Redman deepened his voice like he was scaring somebody. She could tell he was salty by the way his nose had spread clear cross his face.

She knew he could not seriously think as good as she looked. She was just gone stop from going inside to stand out on this cold ass street to talk to his ass. He ain't have it like that! She hated she had gone out the way she did, cause his ass had gotten the big head from it.

"Me? Negro pul-lease! Do you feel this wind? You gots to be joking!" Shuga said, pouting her lips, while stopping to look at him once up, then once down.

"Aye! Nigga with the egg face! Shawty just dissed yo' ass!" Some stud looking chick yelled out loudly to add insult to injury.

"Bitch!"

"Bitch?" Both Shuga and the stud questioned at the same time, not knowing which one he was talking to.

"Don't make me snatch that weave out yo' head hoe!"

Stunned, Shuga just dropped her jaw at how lame Redman had come back.

"Nigga don't be hating on that girl hair." The loudmouth stud told him, then she turned to the crowd saying. "That is a weave, though!"

"Nigga you gone have to bounce," a big ass beefy nigga, who was the club's bouncer, said, just as another equally big ass guy walked up. This one Shuga had never seen working there, but she assumed by his built that he was one of the club's bouncers too.

"You ladies having a problem?" The big ass dude asked, never taking his eyes off Shuga.

"Yeap! We shole is! This old lame ass nigga tryin' to stalk my girl," Kresa said loud and ghetto, pointing right at Redman.

"Ladies, are you all going to come in?"

"We shole will!" Kresa said, smirking while looking over her shoulder at the cold-ass crowd that had probably waited hours to get in and still had not.

Like full-fledged celebrities Shuga and Kresa walked in head held high, not looking back, but hearing Redman cussing and fussing, like the bitch he really was. Kresa tried to ear hustle but could not cause his voice was being pushed farther back. She was a little hot that she did not know what was being said or done. She loved to be on the scene of any action so that later she would be able to pour the juice.

Outside, Redman was leaving, he was smart, he was not gone start nothing he could not finish.

Seconds later, the door flew open, and in rushed, the big dude headed straight their way. "Hello. I'm Chris."

"Shuga," she smiled, revealing her pretty white teeth smile, giving him her hand, which he took caressingly and kissed.

'What the fuck?' Kresa sighed loudly in an attempt to let Shuga know come on. That there were plenty of men, without her acting all thirsty. Check out the rest of the stock first.

Kresa did not like those pretty boy Chris Brown types anyway, and his name would be Chris! All Kresa attempts were in vain, so she popped her tongue hard over Big Bank Black and Kandi's *Get With My Pimpin',* song.

Shuga turned. "Chris, this is my girl, Kresa."

"Yeah. Well, see ya," Kresa said, waving bye with one hand and with her other pulling Shuga's arm that was still interlocked inside of Chris's.

"Do y'all ladies want to chill up in VIP?" He asked just as they were turning about to walk away.

VIP? Tonight? With Da Snowman in the building? That stopped Kresa.

Come with me," he said and lead them to the all-exclusive VIP area.

Kresa walked behind them with a look on her face that Shuga knew. Kresa had that this nigga is fronting look. But she was gone go along with this business of getting them in the VIP just so she could roast his ass when he could not produce. Kresa lived for checking other folks up. She got off on that shit. They bounced up in the spot that was filled with an overflow of wannabes and groupies. By far, Kresa and Shuga were the hottest. Even Ray Charles could see that shit!

"Where you ladies want to sit?" He asked.

"Where we wanna sit?" Kresa repeated in her head. "Down nigga," but looking around, there were no seats available, and her feet were already hurting from the eight-inch heels she wore.

"You ladies want a table that overlooks the stage? Just pick."

"Sure!" Kresa answered loudly! We wanna see the stage!" She screamed out, not hiding the fact that she was alley. She was so ready to get in his shit that she had started sweating... or maybe Kresa was sweating cause she'd half bathed. She was, in her head, mimicking Chris's arrogant ass voice, *'Where you ladies want to sit? Do you ladies want a table that overlooks the stage? Just pick!'* Nigga knew he was flexed up.

Chris left them and walked over to a table of five while they waited. "Shuga, you know this nigga is fronting!"

"Why you say that?" Shuga responded like she had no clue of what Kresa was talking about.

"He trying too hard! Bitch we need to chill out and go find us some real ballers."

"Ladies!" Chris yelled over the noise. When they looked over, the group was gone.

"I know this nigga did not pay them folks to move. Why is he trying to floss so hard?" Kresa whispered behind in Shuga's ear.

"I don't know. Ask him!" Shuga said, loud enough for Chris to hear.

And he had!

"Ask me what?" Shuga smirked while taking the seat opposite of Kresa. Shuga was ready to hear how this bitch was about to go out.

"I was wondering," she laughed lightly, trying to play it off. I was just wondering how you got them, people, to move." Shuga just stared at her fronting ass.

"Tonight, this about my boy. He the man of this shit. I can have all these hoes out... It's too crowded for VIP, anyway? Most of these folks won passes from V103 with that big give away. What you want them to go?"

"N'all Boo, they straight-"

"Whose your boy?" Kresa interrupted Shuga, knowing he could not have been talking about Da Snowman, just as a waitress brought over two bottles of Dom Perignon. "What you work here or something?"

"Something like that," was all the reply Kresa got as she waited on more information but got none.

Chris and Shuga were instantly lost to one another, while Kresa sat around looking lost. "Y'all I 'ma go mingle around," she said, after a while to the air, cause the new couple were acting like they'd found love in the club, talking, laughing, and touching. They were so into each other that either they did not hear Kresa or pretended they didn't hear her. *'I gotta get away from this fake ass shit,'* Kresa thought bitterly.

Kresa walked off pouting but was on a mission, unlike Shuga playing herself, getting caught up with the first lame ass nigga that pressed up on her. She ain't put all that time into looking this good for nothing.

Kresa walked out of VIP sullen, then to make the night that started out hers, but u-turned even worse, she saw Eric, and he was not alone.

Foolishly, for some unknown reason, she felt disrespected as she turned into a watcher - watching him like he was part of the entertainment that everybody had stood in that long line all cold to see. She continued staring all the way to the bar.

"I told you to take yo' ass home, and act like a fucking momma," Kresa heard Eric yelling at Erica over Beyonce singing about putting a ring on it.

"She damn shole did, need to go home to all them kids." Kresa agreed. But at least they were arguing, and that made her feel ah little better.

Kresa hopped on a stool that was a few feet away from them and was about to continue ear hustling when she was pushed hard. On the verge of falling, rough hands caught her.

"What up, baby?"

Kresa jerked away from the unknown grip.

It was a dude with a fucking s-curl trying to fake the good hair look and was all up on her like he knew her.

"Damn! Can a bitch breathe?" Kresa said silently.

She did a quick look over and inventoried him and came up empty. Everything he wore was either cheap, fake, or old.

He eased his way back up on her and began touching her hair. "I like this. Um huh. I like this," Like his opinion really mattered.

Kresa moved away. "Oh shit! What the fuck?" She screamed as her nose was assaulted. "What the fuck is that smell?"

"Huh? A smell? You smell something? What it smells like?" Dude said, and with each word, the smell got stronger. "I don't smell nothing, but this Power cologne, by my boy Fifty Cent that I got on. You smell it?"

The only smell being emitted was hot breath.

"Yeah, this, my boy shit!" No, he did not just get excited. "Look a here," he said, once again invading her personal space while flipping through his cheap plastic wallet to reveal a picture of Fifty and him, side by side.

Kresa could not believe this nigga had really went down to Macy's and gotten that free picture taken with Fifty when you bought a bottle of his cologne and had the nerve to be showing it off. She was about to get his ass!

"Dude, it's your breath!"

"My breath?" On the saying of the word breath, the smell sprayed worst.

"Bitch, my breath? N'all you gots me fucked up! That's yo' ass! Ole twice a month bleeding hoe!" He yelled so loud that he caused the attention to leave from Eric and Erica and be passed right to them.

Right as he began his charade, his boy walked up looking just as lame as him in an imposter purple Versace shirt with green glittery money bags all over it and a pair of skintight skinny Girbuad look jeans that were so high they looked like a toddler size 2T. Then, on his feet were knockoff flea Market Air Forces. They exchanged pounds. WTF? They would be boys.

"Ya boy is in desperate need of a mint," Kresa informed something that everyone should have known.

"Bitch, that's yo' leaky pussy ass!" S-curl screamed hysterically. "You ain't even on my level!"

"Why is you scoping me so hard then? Don't scope me! What you need to do is go find you some Scope! ASAP! ASAP!" She laughed, just as her peripheral view caught Erica exiting the party. Instantly, she turned to see Eric clocking her. She smiled, all the way to her eyes, as he pimped over to her and dude with the hot breath.

"Damn! That nigga gots to know his swag's on midnight. The top fucking hour!" She silently said.

"What's the problem, baby girl?"

"This nigga is mad cause I checked his ass!"

"Bitch, stop lying cause you ain't checked shit! Nigga you better get this hoe!" Stank breath said, mirroring exactly what he was: A lame!

"Breath smellin' like he just ate two buckets of raw chitlins back to back!"

"Man fuck that bitch! Girls are like buses, miss one next fifteen one comin'!" His boy sang out, trying to imitate Gucci Mane, but sounding more like Taylor Swift. Super lame and shit breath hi-fived.

"Baby girl, yo' come with me." Eric's voice reminding her of Fabulous, as he pulled her to the dance floor.

The DJ announced that they were about to give the club something special. Da Snowman was about to perform his new hit single, 'I Know Ya Like It Nasty.'

Kresa kept her eyed glued on him in such a way, you would think he had written the song, dedicated it especially to her, and was rapping it only to her.

'I know ya like it nasty. How I go down on ya and eat ya like a fruit basket. Bend ya over and spread them cheeks. Going at ya, till ya knees get weak. Can ya jump on did dick and ride it in first gear?' He held out the mic so all the ladies could answer. Laughing, as one chick fainted, which was probably part of the paid act. *'I' ma Soulja. I never been a chump. One shot of this dick, and I'll have ya drunk. I don't mean to brag. I'm just a nigga with some fye ass head and a mean ass swag.'* Before the song was over, Kresa had excused herself from Eric to the ladies' room to clean herself up. Her panties were just that wet.

Kresa loved every second she had chilling with Eric until Erica made her way back inside the club, and Kresa wondered how she bullied her way through the club's line twice.

Erica was texting, and Kresa looked around and saw Me-Me, Erica's girl was texting as well. That is the reason why she hated Metro PCS. Thanks to them, every credit challenged bitch in Atlanta now had cellular service.

Right then, she knew what was up. This was the same shit she did. Me-Me had texted Erica and reported that Eric had not left the club as planned, but was dancing all around, something he did not do.

"Yo' baby momma bout to crash the spot!" Kresa told him getting somewhere right as Erica, with her big meaty shoulders putting ya in the mind of a football-playing linebacker, appeared looking confused with the chicken neck popping up and down through the crowd as she scanned the club.

Kresa left running, with the excuse she wanted to avoid drama, as fast as her eight-inch hells let her, to the reggae room, checking to make sure she was not being followed. Then, back to the VIP, where she knew Erica could not follow.

They saw the two men coming back and was not nobody even studying Da Snowman. He might have got a glance here or there, but that was about it. Was not nobody tripping off him, and this nigga was just at the Grammy's.

The way that Shuga had set straight up, breast perked out, Kresa knew Shuga had just lied about being straight chilling with Chris's ass. She should have known that they would be in competition about a rap star.

"Bitch don't act like no damn groupie either," Shuga whispered right before they made it on over to the table.

"Me?" Kresa questioned, knowing Shuga could not have been trying to check her. *'A groupie? Whatever!'* She was gone roast her ass, but she ain't wanna show out in front of Da Snowman.

"What's up?" He asked upon approach, clearly checking for Kresa and clearly disappointing Shuga.

Shuga was used to always being the first pick. To save face, she jumped up and grabbed Chris's face. "I'm trying to get out of here. What's poppin'? Y'all ready to bounce? What's up?" He asked, excited at the display of affection from Shuga.

"Sure," everyone said in unison.

Eric, who was alone, once again spotted Kresa as she walked by proudly, leaving with Da Snowman. Eric turned his swag up and walked over to the group. "Yo, Kresa holla at cha boy," he said, expecting her to stop and run just cause he had called her like she usually would, but not this time.

Kresa knew Eric long enough to see that he did not like the scene before his eyes, by the way, a twitch jerked up in the corners of his mouth. Kresa insides, smiled but kept her game face glued.

"That yo' nigga?" Da Snowman smirked in an intimidating, degrading way that kind of hurt Kresa's feelings. Eric was her nigga, but glancing over at him posted up, looking stupid as fuck with big ass attention-seeking Starburst charm that was clearly cubic zirconium and big fat princess cut block earrings. All that fake ass shit that he proudly wore had her embarrassed. Then looking over at Da Snowman with his glazed up 30 carat Snowman charm necklace... She did not even wanna go no; further, she did not have to. He was the truth. She just held her head down and kept walking like she did not know Eric or even see him. Shit it was not her fault. She had been trying for months to give Eric her all and bring that nigga up, cause she could have done it, but all he did was run back to that ghetto girl of his. With that thought, she turned and mugged his ass, right as Bone Crusher's, *I Ain't Never Scared,* began to play.

The song did what it did and got everyone hype, including Eric. "Bitch, so you think you the shit now, cause you walking with his fake ass?" No, he did not try to get loud, calling out the word *fake!* Drawing attention to all his fake shit.

Da Snowman arrogantly laughed as he kept trucking and made it to the door with a little pep in his step. Eric saw them almost running and took that as a sign of weakness. That sign amped him right on up, so high that he rushed Da Snowman, and hit him with a right so hard it knocked him to the concrete... but before he made it completely down, four niggas came up on Eric from the east, west, north, and no doubt da dirty-dirty south. Kresa turned just in time to see his Starburst charm hit the ground, and fake diamonds splashed everywhere. Shuga pulled Kresa away as she started screaming for the dudes to get off of him.

They were tag-teaming him as soon as one would knock him one way, the other would knock him back. Eric did not even have a chance and was not nobody helping him. He slid down as someone tried to grab him back up, but only caught his shirt. Trying to stay down, over his head, the shirt went, and that was his cue to bounce, but somebody grabbed his belt. Good thing it was not real leather, cause the plastic shit snapped in two, sending the dude who had grabbed it back and Eric forward. His unlaced scuffed Tims flew off as he broke his fall, still running from a crawling position. His ex-large two sizes too big jeans slid down, then off, but he kept going trying to make it to the Montè Carlo with the Starburst logo...Not thinking his keys were left in the jeans that he had just made a quick exit out of. A nervous wreck, he got to his car with Chris and the four dudes still behind him. Then and only then did he remember the keys. He slid right under the car and kept sliding and rolling under vehicle after vehicle until the dudes got smart and ran ahead of his ass and had him surrounded.

"Nigga, bring yo' punk ass out!" Chris hollered, then took off his belt and, with the buckle part, began swinging wild under the car.

Da Snowman rolled up in a 2010 triple black Dodge Magnum next to them laughing. "Yo' Big Cee," he yelled. "Let's be out. That nigga pussy!" Chris pulled out his dick and pissed under the Ford Focus that Eric was hiding under.

Eric was shivering and burning as piss ran in his cuts and scrapes from all that rolling around, but he prayed they would just leave. How the fuck had all this shit went down in front of all them people, and ain't nobody tried to help him? And this was his Zone. Zone 3! A single tear dropped from his eye, not from pain, but from humiliation. Here he had gotten whipped out his clothes at the Chameleon Club and was now hiding under a car in someone else's piss. Eric could not believe that Kresa had let them niggas do him like that.

Chapter 7

LA knew his life was gone have to change. He had met the woman of his dreams, and nothing was gone interfere with him keeping her and his happiness. And for once in his life, he could say he felt happy. Rio had turned into a real-life stalker, that refused to give up her attempts of pursuit after only a couple of one night tryst.

Each time he fell back and went that way, he was always ashamed afterward. What he had needed was a strong black *sista*. Someone he could take home to meet his granny without her having a heart attack... Yet, he continued his same actions for flesh seeking pleasures, any guilt that came behind it was ignored right along with reality, until now.

Kat made him feel different. In a good way. Better than ever. Even though his age was young, mentally, he was an old man set in his ways. He was one to never change who he was or what he was doing, cause he never wanted to feel like anyone could tell him what to do, no matter who they were: Kings rule their own, and he was his own ruler!

Never knowing who his real father was, but frequently having that title replaced with different men... sometimes in as quickly as a month had him lost as a child. All those strange men coming into his life, acting the part to impress his momma in the beginning. Bringing all of their different changes, rules, ways, and lies. Shit, he was not accustomed to.

By the time he was ten, he had had enough! So much so that he did not ever want nobody telling him shit.

Right or wrong! LA did not give a fuck; he would teach himself everything he needed to know.

LA thought back on his momma's last words. "I hate you! You ain't never been shit, but a lil' lying bastard. You'll never mount to shit either!" She had spit those words out with so much venom and so much spunk.... where had it all came from?

His momma had not had that much energy in months, better yet closer to a year. Ever since they admitted her to that hospice to die peacefully from her cirrhosis of the liver. Years and years of alcohol abuse had finally caught up with her, taken over, plus gotten the best of her.

Seconds after she'd screamed those hate-filled words, she closed her eyes and never opened them again. LA had never, to this day, told anyone about the conversation that ended her life. He was torn about his mom's reaction to what had been weighing his heart down... his soul... he had originally thought once he told her, let out what he had been holding in that he would be able to breathe. After ten long years, the weight of suffering and loss so strong... too strong for anyone to hold on to. But it had lingered inside of him, growing, festering in his soul.

But she had said she hated him.

He had loved her. All his life he had loved her, throughout all of the pain, misery, and grief that he had to endure, he never blamed her or changed the way he felt about her.

LA had been sixteen, but from that point on, he was ruthless... There was no stopping him. All respect of everyone was lost, all from his momma's lack of parental support to him. She had not loved him or his brother, just the bottle and, at times, those men. His carefree *don't-give-a-fuck* attitude was locked...until he met Kat, who opened him up with the invisible key she possessed. They were so right for each other, having lived through so much of the same lifestyle, they were drawn to each, yet they were oblivious to one another lives before them.

It had not been a week of them knowing each other, and already he was different. Kat was rubbing his soul, caressing him, making him feel whole. She made him believe without a doubt that his love would be returned. He felt safe to give her his all... And that was what he intended to do.

Love her! Love her like he wanted to be loved.

He looked over at his phone as it rang, with you know who, calling and knew he was gone, have to get a new number. There was no way in hell or on earth would he ever let Kat find out what he held in his Pandora's box.

***

Kresa had caught a major attitude that intentionally went unnoticed, as the group made their way to way to the hotel, where Da Snowman and his entourage were staying. In the elevator, Chris and Shuga were all on each other.

They made it to the top floor and went inside the penthouse suite. Everything everywhere looked expensive. Kresa wished she had knew to carry one of her gigantic bags that she used when shoplifting. She would have lifted the what-nots and gave her granny some or rather sold her granny some.

Party pooping Kresa was quiet while everyone else laughed and joked while reminiscing vividly on the night's events. Kresa kept giving Shuga *'the eye'* that got ignored. Kresa knew that Shuga knew how she really felt about Eric and that she did not want them laughing at his expense.

Kresa could not understand for the life of her why Shuga kept entertaining them, laughing with bullshit talk of Eric. She knew at any time Shuga could have changed the subject but chose not to! To Kresa, it seemed like Shuga wanted them to keep dissing her man.

True, this was it. Being with Da Snowman. What she had envisioned in her mind eye earlier and willed to life; how she out of every girl in the club would be the one chosen. Was even a little shocked at how everything fitted into place and unfolded as easy as it had. Like some greater power had read her thoughts, was happy for her for once, and make her wildest dreams come true.

But now looking back, she should have stayed at home and continued watching the real housewives of Atlanta cause it seemed like she had been bamboozled.

"Shawty, What's up with you? Is you over there thinking bout ya nigga?" Da Snowman popped her thick thigh, still laughing.

'Well, damn! How fuckin' funny was that bullshit?' Kresa thought. *'He outta just write a rap about it. He'd get over it quicker.'* She acted like she had not heard him. "What?" She rudely asked, shaking her head, while scrunching her face up, looking ugly. He grabbed her arm, pulling her up on him.

***

Kat woke up to Mineta's running in and out of the house. Being in prison, living around all those different personalities, had taught her to be a light sleeper. Shuga had jumped up early, and been gone, taking advantage of her live-in 'nanny,' but Kat did not mind, because she was getting so attached to her little niece.

Just as she was coming down the steps, she caught a glimpse of Mineta's back running out the door again.

"I'm next door over Shawan's them," Mineta said, rushing, little arms weighed down by whatever she was carrying that Kat could not see.

Kat's prison paranoia kicked in. She wondered how Shuga knew this Shawan, and was it okay to be letting Mineta go inside of her house?

Upfront, Kat did not trust people due to her upbringing of living around so many lowlifes, and to knowingly place a child around a stranger that was capable of who knows what was even worse.

Kat had seen hundreds and hundreds of girls whose charges included some type of charge against a child, from cruelty to starvation, and even disgustingly molestation. And all child molesters don't look creepy and suspicious like their title. Kat knew that firsthand! So, she threw on her shoes to go check out this Shawan.

She got to the door, knocking, and a familiar voice answered, "Come on in!"

'Was that Mineta?' Kat walked in like the voice that sounded like Mineta's instructed and was almost knocked back out from what smelled like forty years of funk. A baby was screaming to the top of its lungs but was barely heard from the TV that was on full blast emitting static.

Shawan's apartment setup was a little different from Shuga's. You could see straight into the kitchen from the living room because of the half wall. Kat saw that Mineta was at the sink and, disregarding the smell, went to her niece, who was washing dishes standing in a chair.

"Mineta, what is you doing?"

"I'm washing Shuga's skillet out before I take it back home."

"What?"

"I had to cook for the kids," she said, looking over her shoulder.

Kat saw it was four more kids who all looked to be under five. "Where they momma?"

"Oh, she had to go get my daddy out of jail," the oldest one spoke.

Kat did not know if it was a girl or a boy; looking at all of them, she didn't know what any of them were. They all had on mismatched clothing, which gave no clue to their gender and all their hair was B'd-B'd up and missing in chunks.

"Auntie Kat, they didn't have nothing to eat, and we got a lot."

"Y'all always have food," another little one said, who was licking the syrup from the plate and kicking its legs, just happy to be feed.

"I just gotta finish this and change the baby, and I might straighten up a little. It smells pissy."

Pissy was not the word! To Kat, it put her in the mind of how the prison's mental health ward had smelled. Kat went and grabbed the baby up who looked to be a week old but smelled several years stronger. The baby was severely malnourished, extremely skinny with some big bulging eyes. Its head was oddly shaped like it had been dropped, and its scalp was white with crusty, big lumpy flakes. Kat dropped the soiled pamper in a plastic bag from Waverly's and asked the oldest to take it to the dumpster.

Kat put the baby girl, now that she knew what it was, in the sink, and filled the basin with water. The baby just screamed and shook like she was going into shock, looking like a wet newborn bird.

Mineta looked over seriously. "She probably don't know what water is."

Kat noticed Mineta was not like Shuga. Mineta was a sweet child with a big heart. The baby had all kind of diaper rash and raw scabs under her neck where Shawan's lazy triflin' ass had gotten into the habit of just propping a bottle up in her mouth every time she cried, and milk would just waste down her neck and rot. Kat and Mineta cleaned the kids up, then tackled the house, making it look presentable with what they had to work with. When Shawan got home with James, who had been arrested from public drunkenness, she did not even utter a thanks.

A few days later, the house was worse than before, and the kids were still wearing the clothes Kat had put them on.

***

Shuga and Chris had made their way to one of the three bedrooms that the hotel's suite occupied. Walking backwards lip to lip, Shuga fell on the bed with Chris between her legs. He helped her out of her clothes, slowly, then neatly folded them on the desktop. Next, he took off, even slower, his clothes doing the same thing with them.

A draft blew, and Shuga felt her walls drying up and her mood leaving as he took his slow time getting to her like he did not want it. Finally, with only his boxers on, he came over to her, pushing her back. Shuga squeaked, liking that rough shit. He licked her from her neck down to her honey that was dripping from not only her tat but the sweet spot that was in between her legs as well. Slowly, but surely, he was working her right. Chris flipped her over and had her big round brown ass in the air. He spread her butt cheeks as he stuck his tongue in her exit only hole and tossed her salad.

Instantly, she got hot and felt she was climaxing from both holes. Holding his face down, she nutted hard.

'Damn,' she gasped silently, eyes buck wild, *that's the best head I done ever got!'* Just as she thought that he laid back looking like he was ready to get that good returned.

Sike! Was not gone happen, Shuga did not go out like that. She was one of them me-me-me type of bitches. So, getting head from her without delivering some major bread was a no-go...Unless she was feeling the dude, and right now, she was not feeling Chris like that.

After a few long awkward moments of them both laying there side by side, Chris realized he was not gone get any deluxe treatment. He figured she just did not do it. He took his boxers off and grabbed a condom. A few seconds later, he was on top of her humping away heavy.

"Wait a minute!" Shuga hollered. *What the fuck was he doing?* "Are you in?" She wanted to laugh. He had been thus far picture-perfect... so this was his flaw. She got in the groove and faked along with him like a pro, so good Pinkie would have been proud.

***

On the flip side, Kresa was scuffing her knees, doing whatever Da Snowman requested. It is a fact that some niggas swag makes them live life in king status.

Da Snowman had already put it in his head that he was gone dog her face out, then beat her pussy up, for being stupid for a lame, then dismiss her.

Kresa was on her knees in a praying position, while Da Snowman towered over her like he was her God with his dick in her mouth, face fucking her, on the verge of a nut, he kept at it faster and faster, his head hitting her tonsils. As he let his babies flow freely down her throat, he tightly gripped the back of her head, forcing her to swallow or choke. When he released the tight hold, he had a couple strips of her multicolored weave tracks in his hand. He threw that shit to the floor.

"Damn! Nigga you pulled my fucking hair out. I just got it!"

He pushed her back on the bed, ignoring her complaints, and Kresa cocked her legs open wide missionary style. He was just about to get a condom when he noticed something was not right. A funky smell had drifted through the air, and it was blowing harder than the heat.

'What the fuck was that funky shit'? His dick shriveled, and he forgot all about the condom. He began an investigation, following the smell.

Like a hound dog, he found it.

It was her!

Instinct had already told him it was her trifling ass. This bitch was so silly. Kresa had a chance with Da Snowman and was not ready. During his initial investigation, he had knelt down, and all Kresa could think was she about to get served up by Da Snowman. Her whole body shook in anticipation as he roughly pushed her legs, parting them like the Red Sea. The smell jumped at him fast. A fish and onion mix! *And she did not smell that?*

"Shawty, what the fuck is that?" He yelled.

"Huh?" Now she was the dumb one.

"Shawty, what the fuck is all them little balls of clay in yo' shit?" He asked, referring to the tiny yellow-beige balls that were actually clumps of tissue from the self-made pad she'd used earlier when she felt a leak coming from her pussy. "Get yo' nasty ass up and get the fuck out bitch!" He snatched her by the leg and pulled her so quick across the room that she did not have a chance to scream before she was out the door.

"Nigga let me get my girl," she yelled, trying to beat down the thick door, but was not heard.

Da Snowman was not opening the door back up. Instead, he just got on the phone and called for the hotel's security, and within thirty seconds, they were walking off the elevator.

"Ma'am, we're going to have to ask you to leave. You are not a guest, and this is a prestigious hotel, and you're disrupting our guests. Atlanta Police Department has been alerted. But if you leave before, APD arrives this whole situation can be avoided and forgotten.

Kresa looked down on the ground at the stuff that had been thrown out and was able to locate everything but her jeans. "My pants is still in there!" She screamed, kicking the door once again. "Punk bitch ass nigga! Calling muthafuckin' twelve!"

This time the two security guards grabbed her, dipped her around, and hauled her to the elevator with her big stanky ass in the air. Once they made it down to the first floor, the APD was walking through the door and immediately took over. Kresa was booked for indecent exposure, disorderly conduct, and assault on Da Snowman plus two counts of assault on the officers.

During all that action, Shuga stayed knocked out. The next day she woke up late and had not meant to. She had shit to do besides laying up. She pushed Chris so hard that he almost rolled off the bed.

"I need you to take me to my car," she said, rushing to the bathroom to check her hair that hadn't been wrapped last night. Shuga had made wrapping her hair the law, and to wake up with bed head was not happening.

She called out for Kresa as she made it to the living area of the suite.

"Everybody gone," Chris hollered back.

Damn! She just left me? I don't know this nigga like that! Trifling bitch!' Shuga said silently. "Yo' boy ain't tell you he was leaving?"

"N'all he had to fly out to New Orleans this morning. He probably took her with him." If they only knew.

"Oh, okay, well, I'm ready," Shuga said, feeling salty, thinking Kresa was about to get money that she should have had access too.

Chapter 8

Quent sat laughing at Ross's do-boy ass, talking about how he let old man Pete gank him for his clothes.

"Nigga! So, you really believe that Pete had the nuts to dress you down to yo' nuts?" Bald-headed Lou laughed, then spanked Strawberry, a stripper, on her big ass, as she sashayed by.

"Nigga yo' ass was wasted-"

"And ya got 'got'!" Lou interrupted Quent. "You know that bitch Shuga slick as oil."

"I don't know why you was all puppy-eyed over her!"

"Been running round here sick! Fool, need to get it together!"

"I ain't think she'd do me like that though," he said, pouting, eyes watering up at Quent and Lou.

"Nigga! Man, the fuck up!" Bald-headed Lou backhanded him in the chest. "And yo' ass be going along with his bullshit," he pointed to Quent. "I see why y'all women be having y'all whipped."

"Nigga what the fuck is you saying? Who whipped?"

"Quent!" He was interrupted when Bree walked into the room. "What's going on?"

Bigmouth bald-headed Lou was never one to keep secrets. "Talking bout yo' sister with her triflin' ass!"

Bree flinched, wondering how Lou had found out Kittie was *'her sister.'* That was not something that she made publicly known. Confused, she looked over to Quent for an explanation. He threw his hands up, claiming he did not know.

That is when once again, bald-headed Lou, with his big mouth ass, came to fill in all the blanks.

"Shuga done left this nigga butt naked and broke! Now he wanna cry over her ass!"

Relieved that it was that trifling sister. For some reason, when it came to Shuga and her shenanigans, Bree could deal, to an extent. But with Kittie, she had zero tolerance.

"He knew what it was when he left with her," Bree told Lou then turned to Ross. "How many years you been chasing Shuga?" Before he could answer she, was drilling him, "and how many years has she rejected yo' ass? She done pushed you to the curb a million and one times, then one day just out the blue, you thought she was bout to be true? You couldn't have thought that!"

"But I'm really feeling her," Ross said, sounding so sincere that Bree could not even be mean to his soft ass. Bree figured for real that he was just the type of man Shuga needed in her life. A man that would look after her financially without all the drama and bullshit plus Ross was not bad looking. She did not know why her sister would not give him a chance. So, Bree just told him that she would talk to her.

"Okay. Fellas, I need to holla at my man."

"Private?" Bald-headed Lou asked, and when she nodded yes, he had the nerve to look offended. "See, man, I wanted to finish this game," he said, lying, snatching up the money he was about to lose, in the crap game like always.

Quent stood up and followed Bree to his office. "Baby, in the mail, I got this letter saying all 2009 Lexus and Toyotas have a recall due to improperly placed floor carpets... So, I looked it up online, and read this family in California had a tragic accident after the floor mat caused the accelerator to get stuck, so see that accident probably wasn't my fault."

"Bree?"

"Well, it's a chance it wasn't."

Quent was half-listening as he pulled Bree into his lap a started unbuttoning her top. "We'll handle it tomorrow," he told her, then covered her mouth with his, while freeing her of the rest of her clothes. She kissed him back forcefully, clearly turned on and in the mood. "You ready to make a baby?" He whispered, pulling his pants down.

Why did he have to say that?

The mood was gone!

"Baby, my head hurts," she said, jumping up, putting her clothes back on.

"Come on."

"No, baby, my head! It's so much pressure! Maybe you need to stop saying that-"

"Saying what?"

"We about to make a baby-" She gave him her most evil look.

"But that's what we trying for-"

Bree cut him off, "Maybe if we just enjoy the moment, it'll happen." She walked out before he could see the tears welling up in her eyes, leaving him confused.

***

Shuga and Chris jumped in his shiny black Range Rover and headed back to the 'W' hotel's parking garage to retrieve Shuga's Charger. On the ride over, Chris popped in Slow Jams Volume 1, acting all lovey-dovey and shit. Shuga, still sleepy, did not want to hear no love songs. Behind his back, she rolled her eyes, and from there focused out the window and prayed that they did not get caught in Atlanta's crazy traffic cause she was so ready to be home.

A good fifteen minutes and three songs later, Chris turned the volume down.

"Shuga, baby?" He sang out

'Baby?' She frowned.

"There's something I wanna talk to you about."

"Um-huh," she said, agreeing but not really wanting to hear shit.

"I don't want you to think there's anything wrong with me because there isn't. It's just that. Well, you see, I'm at a point in my life where I know what I want, and I can go out and get it. You understand that?" She agreed, only because he paused in his conversation, not that she was tuned in.

"Right now, I'm trying to settle down. I know we just met last night, but shit. I think you're perfect for me. More so than any other woman I've ever met, and whatever faults you do have, I'm willing to accept them."

Shuga crooked her head to the left, not believing the words he had just spoke. *Why was he saying shit like that when he did not even know her last name? Talking about she perfect for him! What a duck!*

"You believe in love at first sight?" He asked, and she really did not want to answer any of what she thought was stupid ass questions.

But since he was so persistently waiting, she couldn't ignore him and didn't know how to change the subject, so she simply gave an "I don't know," sounding as if she was really debating.

Amped-up, he continued once again. "Well, that's what I feel." He leaned over to kiss her. She had her door opened before the car could even come to a complete stop.

"Aye," he said as she jumped out of his truck. "What you are rushing for?"

"Oh, sorry, I gotta go get my daughter."

"Daughter?" He slightly frowned.

"Yes! My little girl! You must not like kids?" And she was glad, thinking he would lose interest.

But he burst her bubble.

"Do I like them? Girl, I love them! I bet she beautiful, just like her mom. I can't wait to meet her."

'Did I invite you to meet my child? Cause I don't remember doing so,' Shuga though jaded.

"Wait a minute. Let me use your phone." He asked, and without thinking twice, Shuga handed over her blackberry. A few seconds later, she heard a phone ring. "I dialed my number. I'm going to save your number plus I'll go ahead and save my number in your phone, so you can have it."

Shuga was speechless. Big Cee was going too far. Why hadn't he just asked her for her number so she could have given him a fake one?

"So, let's try to get together later on tonight."

"Ain't you gone be busy 'guarding or whatever it is you do?"

He smiled, then winked, "for you, I'll make time."

Shuga jumped in her Charger and sped out. She picked up her phone and checked her messages. She had two. One was from Mineta pouring the juice, informing that James was outside beating Shawan up and down the block and that she was going over to Kim's their neighbor. The other was from Kresa, saying she was in Fulton County Jail, on Rice Street, and needed bail bond money.

"Jail?" Shuga blurted, then wondered, what the hell had Kresa gotten herself into now. Never in a million tries would she had guessed that it had anything to do with what really happened. She assumed Kresa had left and gone stealing shit and got busted somewhere. All that time, Shuga had thought Kresa was living it up with Da Snowman.

Without further thought of getting Kresa's bond money, Shuga drove on to her apartment after a tiring night. She was glad to finally see Bankhead Highway or Donald Lee Hollowell, whatever they wanted to call the shit these days. To her, Bankhead Highway will always be Bankhead Highway. That will never change. She was headed straight to her place, to her bed; Kim could bring Mineta later. As soon as she turned in their cutoff, James was outside with a belt running Shawan butt naked, around their old ass rusty Ford.

"Heelllp! Somebody help me! Please! Please! Please! Somebody please!" Shawan screamed to the top of her lungs, hysterical, with her big naked cow titties flopping opposite of each other, every time she moved. She was only twenty-two, but there were seventy-year-old women running around with better bodies.

At one point, the whole neighborhood had felt sorry for her and had run James little crack head ass out of the Overlook. *It did not take much!* But not even two days later, she let that nothing ass nigga come right back, and that was three babies ago. One baby does not even be out of diapers before she pregnant again with the next one. And all the kids stay snotty-nosed and/or shitty pampered every time you see their bad asses. And always begging... But they could not help that. They stood in the doorway, holding the new baby who was not no more than a few weeks, too young for a little kid to be holding. That whole scene melted Shuga's heart. It made her wanna go get her child.

Too late!

"Shuga!" Mineta was running at full speed, screaming. Shuga grabbed her up and went into their house.

"Do you see how James is beating Shawan stupid self?" This was Mineta talking. The little girl was getting more grown every day. "Shuga, I do not know what the hell's wrong with that lady."

"Mineta, stop that damn cursing!" Shuga screamed while thinking back to the one time a man hit her. Ain't no way she had ever let a man beat her. If he does it once, he will do it twice. The first time would be on him. If it was to happen a second time, it would have been on her, and she was not having it.

That is why she dogged they asses off the rip and got whatever she could. Interrupting her thoughts was her phone ringing. It was Chris sending her selfies. She wondered why he let people call him 'Big Cee.' That was a fucking joke, but he was a fucking joke. She turned her phone off.

Later for that clown.

But not too much later... Cause Chris was the next Nicole Simpson. She planned to victimize, then disassociate, because after she used him up, he would be dead to her.

She was half asleep when she remembered she really should have popped Mineta's ass for cursing.

Chapter 9

Bree jerked her Lexus to a stop in front of Shuga's project and leaned on the horn. She was not about to get out and leave her car unattended with these people. She did not like fooling up with the bums from this part of town, so she hoped Shuga was ready.

Shuga walked out of the house looking flashy, and Bree wondered why she had not been robbed yet, with all these hoodlums that just loitered around day and night looking to be in search of a victim.

As soon as Shuga shut the door, Bree was all over her ass. "Why'd you do it? I mean, why?" Bree was ready to roast her ass for shit that has been building.

"Why I do what?" Shuga uttered, trying to think while looking dumbfounded. What had she done this time? Really was not no telling.

"Listen here, you little whore, Quent has been all over my case!" Bree exaggerated, as she flew into Bankhead Highway's traffic without so much as a glance to see if she had the right away or not. Automatically assuming she had it like that and that everybody on this rachet road should know. "You shouldn't have done that shit...Ross is good people."

"Ross? OMG! That's why you called me all hysterical and shit? Bitch please!" Shuga popped hard, then relaxed more in her seat.

"Shuga, you did not have to take shit from him. He would have given you whatever you needed. But now, little whore you done fucked that up, cause Ross is a really good dude for real! He would have looked for you."

"See, Bree, you don't understand yet. There is no way you can see what I see and know what I know because you haven't been through nothing. Quent is like your first real man, and you lucked up, like the baddest bitch when you pulled him. Now 'he' is a good dude for real, but all niggas ain't like him. In fact, none are like him. So, don't ever try to compare yo' man to these simpletons, cause that's all I get. I'm used to their asses, though. There's a difference with niggas supplying wants versus needs. A lot of niggas- I take that back! Not a lot-lot, but some will supply needs, but when it comes to wants, they'll say you don't need it. So, I gotta look out for me... Besides, fuck him anyway! I barely got twenty-seven hundred outta his broke millionaire wannabe status ass... I don't wanna hear no more about it."

Bree sighed and rolled her eyes at the look Shuga gave her.

"So, you lied to me talkin' bout you wanted me to help you look for some house rugs? Just so you could get me alone and *'try'* to check me about Ross's lame ass? Puh-lease! I can't believe that shit. That shit is so old anyway!" Shuga said as they pulled up at the Cumberland Galleria Mall.

"No!" I just never had the chance to get at yo' behind about him! But I thought you said you ain't wanna talk about it no more. But he still be checking for you." Bree added quickly.

Shuga rolled her eyes this time, and nonchalantly, she said, "Don't they all."

"Anyway! I didn't just want you to help me look for those rugs, either." Bree got quiet. "No... it's about... well I... I wanted to talk... It's about Quent," she barely managed to get out, and Shuga knew something was up.

"What? He cheating? With who? Come on bitch! Turn around! Let's go to that hoe house right now!" Shuga said, spinning around, ready to head back to Bree's newly repaired Lexus that had just been shined up and was gleaming.

"No! He is not *'cheating'* on me," Bree hoped.

Shuga had just planted a seed in Bree's head that from her own paranoia would take root and grow, but for now, it was just a thought that she just hoped was not true.

Bree took a deep breath and revealed to Shuga the deep dark secret about her hysterectomy that she had been hiding from everyone. The secret that she was in denial about and did not even want to believe herself. Shuga's eyes stayed wide and glued on Bree the entire time.

"You really want to stay with that nigga? You really love him?" Shuga frowned but did not wait for an answer before continuing. "Well, I guess you do. You been with him five long-ass years! *'Damn!'* Four years and three hundred and sixty-four days longer than I would have." She laughed at her own little joke.

Bree did not! This was not a laughing matter, and she did not appreciate Shuga being facetious at a time like this. Bree just continued dabbing her eyes, as tears were her cheeks. Shuga got serious.

"Baby, if the doctors gave you a hysterectomy, it ain't no way possible, that y'all are going to be able to conceive a child naturally. I could think of a couple things, but first, you need to get that nigga to marry you since you wanna keep him. That is the first thing first! Then for the rest of your childbearing years, you could keep faking pregnancies, then cry miscarriage."

Staggered beyond belief, Bree could not believe what her sister was saying but then looked over at Shuga, whose facial expression proved she was dead ass serious.

"Has he ever been locked up?" Shuga was still going.

"I don't think so! No! Why? What does that have to do with anything?"

"Cause if we can get him locked up for about four or five months. You know you could buy a baby from one of them teenage hoes that live by me. It's about fifty of um under twelve pregnant. They fast asses don't want no baby for real. Young sluts be just fucking raw and getting pregnant."

"What?" Bree crooked her neck but did not complain. Could not! She had asked for Shuga's help. She should have known it was gone be the lowest of the low, straight from the gutter type advice that anyone could possibly give, and she was the dummy for entertaining it.

"Yeah, bitch! That'll work right there. That's the plan," Then, she repeated in detail like it was all good. "See, we get his ass locked up for a few months. You tell him you been put on bed rest, doctor's orders, and can only talk to him on the phone. So, you ain't gotta go see him. We go offer one of them half grown hoes bout five G's, and they'll give a baby up. Probably way less. You dark. He light. So, it don't even matter what color the baby comes out. He come home! He have a baby! But first thing, first! Get him to wifey yo' ass da real way! You gotta do that, but don't worry, boo! Big sis here for you. We gone get you a baby. That ain't no problem, don't worry bout that!"

Bree just nodded her head absently at her insane sister, hoping no one had overheard their conversation that should have been private but was done openly in the public mall.

***

Times flies quickly when you are having fun, and Kat was having the time of her life. It had been four whole weeks since they met, and time had done its thing and flew by. It seemed like only yesterday when LA had the wreck and picked Kat up off that corner. But now, a whole month later, they were still inseparable, wanting to sing out along with Alicia Keys when she was screaming about that unbreakable love. Shuga was not hating hard, expecting Kat to be at her beck and call. She was mad at because she had expected her to be Mineta's live-in babysitter. When Kat did not show back up after her first weekend out, she was fye-hot! She had even been tempted to throw out all her prison belongings.

Shuga, first mind told her that Kat had relapsed and was back on that shit. Little did she know, Kat's life was on fleek. Doing what Shuga wished she could be doing. Once Shuga found out what was really up with Kat, she could not believe everybody had a man but her. *What was really going on?*

LA loved to shop, and soon he had Kat feeling the same way. He had taken her to every mall, store, and shop he could think of. She was buying so many clothes that they would have them delivered instead of lugging everything all around with them. He took her everywhere with him! Places she had never been and never thought of going. They did everything together, and he tried to show her off, whether they were going to dinner, the movies, or dancing. And he did not even dance, but anywhere she wanted to go, he was with it. She had never been to Six Flags, so he took her there the day he found that out.

"How is you from the 'A,' born and raised, but ain't never been to Six Flags? Shawty come on," he couldn't believe that shit. "What have you been all yo' life?" He asked, stunning her.

Did he really want an answer?

Kat could never look him in his eyes and reveal her past. She was ashamed more than anything. Good for her, he was joking, and his question had been somewhat rhetorical.

The thing that Kat loved about LA more than anything else was, he never asked her about her past. Not about family. Not about anything that could link her to who she used to be. All he cared about was the here and now.

In a funny way, it was like he was helping her secrets to be just that. A secret.

Unknown to Kat, LA liked the same thing about her. She was not all nosey, wanting to know who all he had been with and this, that and the third. She did not delve all up in a nigga's life. All she cared about was how he made her feel and what was going on with them now.

That is not something he could tell her, though, to tell her that would then make things appear artificial like he had something to hide... Which he did, but he did not want her to have suspicious thoughts. That would make her investigate exactly what he wanted no one to know. So, things would remain, she told him what she wanted him to know, when she wanted him to know and how she wanted him to know, and he did not question anything. In return, he gave her that same respect. Truly, to Kat, it did not matter what LA had done in his past, cause everyone has the right to change and grow, and others have the right to accept it or move on.

Their relationship was very comforting. Anywhere LA went, he was cool with Kat knowing and going if she wanted to. They went so many places together that their shared joke had even become *'if I go to jail, I'm taking you with me.'* It is crazy after Kat doing five real years locked up that she could even begin to joke about something as serious as that. But that's how LA made her feel. He gave her hope, and life had new meaning for her now.

***

Shuga jumped up, scared from the beeping of the apartment's fire alarm. Heart racing, she instantly rushed down the steps to find Mineta with a chair at the stove. "Girl! I was hungry! But this pan won't stop smoking," she said, waving black smoke that was circling with her hand.

Shuga jerked Mineta down, out of the chair and pushed it to the middle of the room, so she could stand in it to turn the alarm off. Only it was too much smoke, and as soon as it would go off a few seconds later, it would be right back beeping.

Irritating her with its loud squealing. She looked over at Mineta, who was standing hand on hips like she had not done anything wrong.

"Mineta, I'm gone beat yo' ass, for real this time," she said, removing the batteries from the alarm.

"Beat my ass?" Mineta's big green eyes popped, questioning. "Beat my ass for what? I just said I was hungry. You ain't cooked!"

"Why you didn't just eat bologna?"

"I did! But I wasn't gone eat that stuff raw. It be all slimy and wet. You been sleep all day, and I was starving. What was I supposed to dooooo!" Mineta got all her smart comments out, then started crying.

"OK, OK," Shuga could not handle Mineta crying, and Mineta used that to her advantage.

From her own life growing up unhappy, without a mother, she always tried to comfort Mineta, but it was done in a superficial way. The only thing Shuga knew was to buy her things. She thought that would make Mineta happy and complete. Shuga remembered all the days she wished for a momma and hoped that she could have nice things like the other little girls. She thought back to when she was twelve. Even though this is something that is never aired, but she remembered. Kat, well, Kittie back then had stopped going to school and started bringing money in. Shuga was so tired of wearing the same clothes that she was gone go work with Kittie doing whatever she was doing, but when she approached Kittie with the idea, it was rejected. Instantly, Shuga assumed even though Kittie was helping her sisters that she knew if Shuga made her own money, she would be the flyest of them all. Following Kittie, one day, she saw what Kittie was sacrificing just to feed them. *Herself.* Shuga knew she would never walk up and down the block selling her body to different men, just to feed them. She never mentioned seeing her and never talked about work again.

Shuga proceeded to finish Mineta's bologna sandwich; she just wanted to do her best with Mineta. Her thoughts of just how she was going to do that were interrupted by a knock at her door.

She went to answer it, and there stood an FTD florist delivery guy. "Delivery for Shun'te' un Mason." He extended two dozen multicolored roses with a card attached.

Since she was not much of the flower type, immediately she threw the arrangement and went to the card, hoping it contained cash. Opening the card, walking back to the kitchen, Mineta had the chair pulled up to the counter with a butcher knife about the size of her arm about to slice a tomato.

"Mineta!" Shuga screamed, scaring Mineta and causing her to jump and lose her footing.

In an instant, Shuga dropped the card and dashed to Mineta, who was falling with the knife still in her hand.

Not a second too late, Shuga caught Mineta by her arm and scooped her up. The knife fell, then ricocheted, then fell again, this time bloody.

"Baby, are you alright?" Shuga asked Mineta, who was screaming once again.

She sobbed out a *'yes'* but continued bawling.

"Baby," Shuga talked smoothly. "It's OK. I'm sorry for yelling at you. Where are you hurt?" She asked, breathing heaving, adrenaline-pumping hard.

Mineta lifted her hand palm up, revealing the blood that had leaked on them.

"Mineta, where is you cut at tell me now?"

Mineta shook her head. "I'm not Shuga, but you are." She said, pointing to the long gash on Shuga's thigh.

"Oh shit!" Shuga said, all at once, getting her senses back. Her legs had been perfectly markless, and now she wondered how bad a scar this would leave.

She grabbed a towel and Mineta's arm and ran out the door right as Chris was walking up.

Startled, she jumped. "Shuga, did I catch you at a bad time?" Under normal circumstances, Shuga would not be caught running out the house in no cut off jean shorts with a head rag tied on her head. But these were not the norms. First, she had just gotten cut, but more importantly, Chris was a joke to her, and she did not care how she appeared to him. Because in her book that mattered, he did not count. She was so agitated, she did not think to question, *'How in the world did Chris know where she stayed?'*

"Yes! I have to get the hospital," removing the blood-soaked dish towel.

"You're hurt!" He grabbed Mineta up. "I'll drive y'all."

Shuga did not know why she had directed him to Grady, a ghetto charity hospital. She wondered that after he asked at registration how much it would be. She could have gone anywhere. She should have known he was gone offer to pay. But of course, the bill would really be going through Peach care, Georgia state Medicaid, but he did not need to know all that.

"Oh well. I don't know yet," she said, sighing, turning her attention to Mineta. "Baby, are you still hungry?" Mineta just stared like the answer should have been obvious. That little girl had a way of sometimes being so unpredictable with her funny acting ways.

"Yes!" Finally, Mineta screamed with the attitude of a sixteen-year-old. "I shole am hungry. My stomach is touching my back," she exaggerated. Shuga should have known this was coming. "Have I even ate today?" She asked no one in general but embarrassed the hell out of Shuga as it was almost five. The nurses and Chris had heard, all she had to do was say yes or no, did not nobody ask her to add all the extra shit.

"We were cooking when I got hurt, remember?" She asked, but did not let Mineta answer, quickly she turned to Chris. "Chris, will you take her to the cafeteria while I finish up here?"

"Sure," he said too fast with no hesitation, which would have made the average parent leery.

Shuga didn't care, neither did she think twice about using her daughter to get rid of Chris, nor did she think she could be putting Mineta in harm's way by allowing her to go off and be alone with a strange man, that she herself had only known a few hours. All Shuga's mind could fathom was her scheme of the moment. She only wanted Chris to be gone so that she could come up with some type of bill. Her focus was on this stack or two that she should be able to get out of him.

The bleeding had stopped, and she was given twelve stitches. She could tell a small scar would be left, and that would take away from her legs flawless beauty.

That dropped another bomb. She figured it would not hurt to try to get Chris to spring for some plastic surgery. A surgery she may or may not get. More than likely, when vanity took over, she would, but she would lie and say it cost three or four, maybe ten times as much as it really did. That way, she would be able to walk away with a little something out the deal.

"This bill gone be high as hell," she said once they were back, and the doctor had left. "Plus, there is no telling how much the medication is gone be."

"Shuga, I told you not to worry about nothing. I got you. I brought my card with me."

A Card? That is not what Shuga wanted to hear. "Oh, no! Since you, not my husband, they not gone, take no insurance card."

"No, I meant my credit card."

"Nope! Not that one either," She lied. Of course, they would take a credit card payment, as long as the card was good. The problem was she could not take a credit card payment.

"But there's a Bank of America nearby. You could get cash. Wait, it's a ATM on the first floor somewhere if your card allows cash advances. Does it?"

"Yes! What do you think the bill is gone run?"

"You might need bout fifteen, but at least bring two."

The lie rolled off Shuga's pretty lips smoothly.

"Two thousand?" Chris repeated, and Shuga assumed she had asked for too much.

'Damn', she thought. "Why am I always being greedy."

Then he said. "That's all? I got that on me now," pulling out a gwap that consisted of nothing but Benjamin's.

Relieved, she smiled her million-dollar smile that could melt iron, while silently sending thanks to God for putting this lame in her lane. Then she frowned, thinking 'damn it,' she could have asked for way more. Now she had to once again get his ass out the door, cause ain't no way, they were paying a hospital bill. Not happening. Her body shivered at the thought.

"Baby, what's wrong? You shaking. Are you cold?" He said, removing his Sean John velour sweatsuit's jacket, showing off his muscled, tatt'd up chest that was only covered by a black wife beater.

'Damn, he was fine!' Shuga stared. But that was it cause a little dick she could never work with!

Chapter 10

"Wet! But it can get wetter, wetter, wetter! I'm calling you, daddy! 'Daddy! Daddy! Daddy!',"* Mineta sang along with the girl on Twista's song, emphasizing daddy each time loudly.

Embarrassed cause of who they were rolling with, Shuga turned around and glanced at Mineta like she was crazy. Mineta missed the look, meaning to silence her; instead, she winked like what she was doing was all good.

"Um-um! Don't be singing that! Where you heard that at?" She asked, pushing the c.d. in that was hanging out to change the sexual song.

Mineta began fussing about it being on the radio all the time right as *'Let's Get It On!'* by Marvin Gaye boomed out of Chris's speakers.

"Ohh!" Mineta screamed with it, snapping her fingers. "That's my song!"

"Girl, I am so sick of you! What station was that?"

"Hot 1-" Before Chris could get it out, she was making him turn it to V103, just in time to hear Ms. Sophia with girl talk on the Frank and Wanda show.

Chris was quiet through the exchange that took place between Shuga and Mineta. As soon as he turned into Shuga's apartments, he was stopped by neighborhood kids blocking him, that were getting wet from the water hydrant they had busted open. Shaking his head, wondering where the parents were and thinking how sick they were going to be, considering it was a winter day even if the sun was out. He blew his horn at them, but they did not move an inch. After all, this was their block, and he was the intruder. He could get his ass on.

Shuga half jumped out of the car, screaming. "Why is y'all blocking the street? Move y'all little rotten asses on! Can't y'all see a car coming through? Y'all dumb asses gone get hit!"

Shuga got shown no respect, they did not listen to their own momma, why would they listen to her.

"Fuck you bitch!" A six-year-old thug in the making who belonged to her neighbor Linda retorted.

"Yah, fucs yau bits!" Followed by his three-year-old Jr., The brothers both grabbed their privates in disrespect, continuing to curse, but moving out the way. When Chris was passing them, the boys tried to kick the truck.

"Ms. Linda need to do something bout them nappy-headed lil' boys of hers. They ain't gone mount to shit." Mineta said, dipping to the front.

"Mineta! What I tell 'you' about 'yo' badass mouth?"

"Shuga," she said calmly. "I'm just telling the truth, though. Me and Kim was talking bout that just the other day," she let her know before sliding back in the seat.

"Have you ever thought about moving?" Chris said in a tone that showed he was clearly disgusted and was now acting uppity as if he was better than what he looked around seeing.

Shuga clearly did not care what he thought of 'where' she lived, because she knew 'how' she lived. Once she got into her apartment. She did, however, envision another lucrative opportunity. She was gone get way more than a funky two-thousand dollars outta his ass. He acted like he had it like that... well, he was about to prove it!

"Yeah, I've thought about moving. I think about it every day. But the fact of the matter is it's gone be hard to jump out and do something like that. Right now, here, is all we can afford. I don't have no help. Mineta's daddy been missing since I told him I was pregnant"

"He shole have, but if we find him, we gone take his ass to the child support place. Ain't that right, Shuga?" Mineta leaned upfront interrupting with her big apple green eyes glistening. Mineta's beauty at the tender age of six already had strong influences. No one could stay mad with such a cute little girl, no matter what she did or said.

"Mineta go and open the door and gone in the house. I'll be there in a minute."

"Humph! Well, gimme the key then!" Mineta snatched them out of Shuga's hand, then slowly got out of the truck, slammed the door, and walked off with an attitude. She was mad cause she wanted to be included in on all the conversation. All the other adults talked around her, and she had gotten used to that. So much so, that at times she did not even like to talk to kids her own age.

"Chris, I don't know what I'm going to do," she said, looking around, not really noticing anything wrong with her neighborhood.

Chris was just too uppity and arrogant! He had a fucking big ass ego and a little 'ha-ha-ha,' she thought. He needed to be brought down a notch or two. There was no way Shuga was giving up a place that offered free rent, plus they sent her a four-hundred-dollar check, once a month for her utilities. Nope, not happening. She was not about to lose all that just to go pay rent in no unseen neighborhoods living around white folks. *Pay rent? Yeah right!* She was straight, but of course, she was not gone tell him that. She would act like she hated the neighborhood as much as he did. He got out the truck and walked around to the passenger side door, where he picked her up and carried her into her apartment.

"I don't know how I'm gone make it to work tomorrow," she lied. *Work? She had gotten so dramatic lately.* "You see how all these unpredictable events keep coming into my life? This," she pointed to her leg, "Is going to cost me to get behind on my bills."

"N'all, don't even worry bout that. You know I got you."

"Chris, I don't want you to feel like you owe me anything. We just met and-"

He cut her off. "Yeah, I know, but like I told you. I'm settled, and I've never met anyone like you. You got me where I wanna stay. I'm going to help you out. Don't even worry about work.... tomorrow."

Shuga had wanted him to tell her she had no worries, but why had he put a time limit on it?

'Tomorrow?'

"Let me use your bathroom," he asked, standing just when Shuga noticed his wallet had slid out of his sweatpants and was laying in plain view on her couch.

Shuga walked upstairs to see what Mineta was doing, who was in her room, knocked out cold in front of the TV. Shuga tiptoed back down the steps with no bounce cause she knew Mineta was a light sleeper.

It is like her little ass never wanted to miss nothing, and sleep would make her do just that, miss, something! Besides, Shuga did not want her fast ass all up in her mouth. Chris was back on the couch when she returned, so she put a little limp in her step and winced like she was barely making it.

"Baby? Does it hurt when you walk?"

"Only a little," she said, stopping to sit in his lap. Then, she realized that he too musta noticed his wallet had fallen out because she now felt it back in his pants.

"Like I said, I'm going to get you all out of here."

Shuga sighed to him but smiled on the insides. She was loving this! She had to remember to thank Kresa's hating ass for suggesting they go to Club Chameleon that night.

Speaking of Kresa, Shuga had forgotten all about her being in jail! But she was sure somebody had bonded her out by now, cause if not, Kresa would have been blowing up her phone like whoa. And she had not called back once!

Shuga did not think that the only way Kresa could call was through a three-way, cause she been put that collect call block on her phone, back when Mark had gotten locked up a while back and would not stop calling her. He just kept calling like it was some type of mistake that every time he dialed her number, the operator told him his call was not accepted.

Chris stood and told her they could go look for a place tomorrow. Once he was gone, Shuga slid out the credit card that she had swiped out of his wallet, then frowned. *'A black American Express card? What the fuck!'*

She hoped the shit was some good cause she was rushing, so he would not catch her and had not noticed what Shuga had pulled out, and she had never seen one of those before.

In her heart, she knew deep down if she asked for something, Chris would more than not give it to her. But um-um! To her, it felt better to take what she wanted, especially from bustas like him.

***

Never had life been easy, and the fact that everything was going so smoothly for Kat scared her. She was actually in a real relationship. Never in life had she had anyone to show her love. She did not know whether she should tell him she loved him or hide the way she felt. Kat wanted so badly not to hold any secrets from LA but was lost. She wanted to open her heart to him because it felt like she was lying to him, and that is something she never wanted to do. They had a connection. He liked her. 'Her' being the person she was today.

'Would he still want her if he knew the truth?'
Never had she been anyone's main girl. Always the sideline hoe or worse.
'Would her past be held against her?'
That was a question she was unsure of. Therefore she decided she would do right for herself by keeping her past left behind, even though she was not that person anymore.

Kat had been afraid that LA's brother Monty would remember her, but it just so happened that last year he had been killed in a motorcycle accident. So now, there was no connection to LA that could enlighten him about all the horrible things she used to indulge in. She felt like that was confirmation from the heavens to keep what was in the dark in the shadows and far away from him. He was her man, and she did not want anything to change that.

Kat looked over at LA, and a superior feeling of greatness overcast her. A feeling that she wanted to be with him forever and could be with him forever.

Kat was always like that. Anybody who showed her a little attention, she latched on to them. She confused that feeling with love and would instantly fall in lust with them. It started out with people but turned to drugs. That misconception was developed due to her upbringing, where she was neglected and lacked love. Even before her momma got caught up in the street life, she never paid her girls any attention or love. Kat tried to show Shuga and Bree love, but by her being the oldest, no one showed her love.

All this seemed unreal for Kat. She had not been out of prison a month, and already life was looking up. She had found a good man, and everyone was hating. Especially Shuga. She did not like it at all. Secretly, Shuga wondered why she had never run into LA. She ran in the circle of all the paid men but had never heard of him. And that was weird because she knew everybody upfront personally or had heard of them. But this LA was new to her scene. She hated on Kat every chance she got, always fussing, telling her that she was moving too fast and that LA was probably using her.

"Using me? For what? I don't have shit!" Kat had said, unbelieving Shuga, wondering why after all she had endured, why she just could not be happy for her?

Shuga's response was, "Dummy! He gone have yo' ass moving dope or some shit, and next, you'll be back using it." Shuga loved to throw that up in her face. Then, she went on to tell her she would be back locked up, sitting in prison, and where would he be? Gone, out fucking the next skeezer!" Shuga did not never have encouraging words to say about her relationship.

Kat was so lost in her thoughts, contemplating her past and future, that she did not notice her present. LA had pulled up in front of a house that she was all too familiar with.

What the fuck were they doing at Turk's trap? No, this could not be happening! Scenes invaded her mind's eye of five years earlier. Panicking, Kat turned to look at the house in depth. There were a couple kids running around, and the outside of the once dingy fading blue house had been upgraded with some cheap white vinyl siding. Relived, nothing looked the same. She exhaled, but that breathes was caught in her throat when she saw who came to the door to meet LA.

"Kat, I want you to meet my boy, Redman."

'Redman! Redman! Redman!' The name ring loud in her ear. "Redman, this Kat, my baby."

"What's up?" Redman was stuck, looking at Kat, who had quickly turned her head. Still, he studied her profile in amazement.

Smiling broadly and showing off them sixteen golds, LA took Redman staring as gawking, cause in his eyes, Kat was that bitch! Flirting never failed with Redman; he was always like that, always trying to charm every girl he met. But not this time. 'Flirting,' in his usual joking manner, was not on the agenda. He was wide-eyed and had actually gone into a mild shock behind who LA was claiming as 'his' girl.

Redman, could not believe ole crackhead ass Kittie had cleaned up. The last he had heard, she was in prison for that bullshit she'd pulled the night Turk would not sell to her. He had felt some 'deep six' shit was about to go down. His momma always warned him to be aware of your gut feelings. Following her, OG advice is what had kept him alive and from being in jail fighting football numbers. He had left only minutes before she had arrived.

Redman had not known when Kat was supposed to have gotten out of prison or that she ever had. But it was not like he cared either; as long as she kept her trifling ass away from his shit, he would continue to care less. Besides, he was never one to inquire about the status of one's wellbeing anyway. If it did not include him or involve him in some type of way, he had two words: *Fuck it!*

Prison had done Kat well; he could tell that just at a glance. No longer did she look like a skeleton zombie with big popped eyes that were always searching around. If her banana yellow skin, green eyes, and light blond hair were not so distinguishing on a black person, he probably would not have even known who she was. Cause she did look good, and that was what was different about her.

But everything that looks good ain't always good for ya, and he knew about her stank ass. He wanted to laugh in this niggas face. He could not believe that LA, with his big-time gwaped up ass... the way he portrayed his life was messing with a crack monster.

LA hustled hard and had come up in the game quick, being led by his older brother, Monty. At a young age, he learned all the tricks and trades that came along with hustling in the streets. From dealing with not only shiesty niggas and bitches that are supposed to be on ya team, but also ruthless fiends that will cut ya throat for a few pennies. Then when Monty was killed unexpectedly in an accident, in a matter of mere minutes, shit changed forever. LA had to handle all that was left to him. He did not have choices. So, not even taking a day off to grieve, he picked right back up where his brother left off and continued running the family business.

LA ruled with an iron fist; he was taking no lost, and never played with their ass, demanding respect from all the ole school cats who mattered while his power continued to grow rapidly.

True, LA was still young, liked to be seen, played around but choose to judge him off that alone. You would find yourself missing only to be later found floating face down stanking. LA had calmed down, surprisingly, with the increased power that he now held cause before, he was a fool with it. Back in his teens, he would walk straight up on niggas that had beef just to blow their brains to smithereens in broad daylight. He loved the king role he inherited from Monty and felt it should have been his all along.

"Nigga, stop staring at my baby!" He had pulled Redman to the side. "I just wanted you to meet the one that might be her. We'll holla." LA threw the deuces.

"N'all-" Redman was about to say but was cut short by LA's actions. Looking like a sucker, he was all smiles jumping around, acting like a lovesick puppy.

Redman could not do nothing but shake his head at Kittie, who had done a triple take on him, surprised, with what he recognized as fear in her eyes. He remembered how he had passed on fucking her cause three little letters, H.I.V, did have him scared. But not his boys. Almost every one of them fucked her for a hit. He thought back to how they had to get her putrid-smelling stanking ass out the house after Melvin had nutted up and beat her half to death. They had thrown her naked body in the trunk and dropped her off at Grady hospital, not knowing if she would make it through the night. Not caring one way or the other, she just had to go cause they was not have no bodies making their trap hot. Then she had pulled through only to return with the same shit, getting high and tricking off like nothing had happened. She'd fuck and suck anything for a few crumbs.

Redman looked at her in disgust, was not no telling what kind of venereal diseases that hoe had contracted. LA had better be careful cause that hoe was out there.

LA made his drop and, as promised, headed out to the Stone Crest Mall, twenty minutes east of Atlanta, where he was set to take Kat shopping. Only Kat's excited mood had long faded, back at Turk's.

Now dizzy and overwhelmed, she was seeing stars all around her, she was sweating heavily and on the verge of passing out. She looked like she had just hit some bad dope.

***

A man of his word Chris called later that night to remind Shuga, who needed no reminder, that they were going to look for her new apartment in the morning. First thought, when she had got the call was, he had noticed that his credit card was missing, and she was prepared to deny all. He had no proof it was her anyway.

Shuga was one that never paid attention when her foster mom came from church preaching on how you reap what you sow. Or how her very first drug-dealing boyfriend, even with the type of enterprise he was in, always said be fair to others, because *what goes around comes around.* That just made her take him as lame, and within a week of him telling her that dumb ass shit, she had him set up to be robbed. She was not a believer in you *'Get It How You Live It.'* She never thought with all the *'get'* she got, that one day there had be some *'get back.'* She would not waste a moment's thought entertaining that a wrath could be sent her way. Her only focus was hitting the next big lick...and those licks kept coming. And while she sat at her house doing nothing, one came to her; the first part was executed simply when she answered the phone.

"Listen, Chris, I really want to thank you for what you're *'trying'* to do and how you're *'trying'* to help me and my daughter with a better life, but I don't know. Right now, this apartment right here is all we can afford-"

Chris interrupted her, "I told you, don't worry about the money. I got you."

'I'm sure you do,' Shuga thought, sarcastically. *'But who got you?'* She needed to know who had him. To know that information would give her insight on how much he had her.

Chris had originally led Shuga to believe that he was a bodyguard for Da Snowman, but that could not be true cause he was never guarding him. So, she did not know what his ass did. She chalked him up to be a fronting ass nigga who was only boys with Da Snowman. Probably from way-way back in the day.

Therefore, he looked out for him. It did not matter exactly what he did for income. As long as he kept her pockets fed, she would get all she could get. But after everything he had to give was gone, she was cutting this shit short. Shuga ain't like messing with wannabes, cause when they went broke, and she got ghost they could not handle it. And she definitely did not need another stalker-like Mark's broke ass!

Not even one single time did Shuga think of the fact that this nigga was walking around with a black American Express card issued to him. There had to be more to him than what meets the eye. Even the good Dr. Scott did not have exclusive memberships offered to him like that.

But those thoughts never dawn on her. Shuga assumed that platinum was always the best, so she assumed that the platinum American Express was the best too.

Shuga did not like how Chris had interrupted her spiel. She had more shit to say. "Like I was 'saying'! You might have me this month, but what about next month or the one after that or even next year? When we're living it up and done, forgot about this side of town. I miss one month cause I can't afford it, then what? I lose everything." What she wanted this man that she had just met to say and mean was that he had her for the rest of her life.

Shuga ain't never foresee a future without playing lames.

"How about this? I can do this for you-" *'Ding-Dong!'* "Once we find you somewhere to move-" *'Ding-Dong!'* "A real nice safe neighborhood, then I will-" *'Ding-Dong!'* "pay about a year in advance. So, rent will not be a worry."

"Wait a minute. I do hear everything you is saying, and I'm listening but hold up somebody at my door."

"Is everything alright?" Chris asked anxiously. "Do you need me to come over?"

"N'all it's just my sister. I been waiting on her," she lied.

"What's up bitch!" Ray'neisha screamed as soon as Shuga opened the door, looking busted. One day Shuga was going to ask her what she did with all the money she made, cause ole girl did not ever fix-up.

Ray'neisha was another chick Shuga fucked with on the credit card tip. After calling Kresa's phone several times with no luck, she blew her off and called someone else. *One monkey don't stop no show.* Never once thinking that the girl could still be in jail and may need help herself.

Shuga motioned with a finger for Ray'neisha's alley ass to be quiet.

"Chris, I'm back. I let her in. Soooooo. You'd do that for *'meee'*?" She made her voice sound sweet and humble.

"Baby, you ain't even got to ask nothing like that. You know I'm trying to make you the one. It ain't nothing I wouldn't do for you. Baby, you ain't ever gotta wonder."

Why he tell her that? She loved it when a nigga told her, *'you can have whatever you like.'* If Chris could see her big goofy grin, he had thought she had been serenaded by T.I. himself.

"What time are you picking me up to go house hunting?" Not apartment looking but house hunting! Shuga had upgraded.

"Eight-" He said and was about to say more.

"Aight. I'll be up and ready." Shuga was so excited she hung the phone dead in Chris's face without any ending pleasantries.

"Bitch!" Shuga screamed, turning to Ray'neisha, her real voice back. "Don't you ever bring yo' alley ass up in the place where I rest my head with all that loud ghetto ass shit, and you saw I was on the phone."

Ray'neisha sucked her teeth. "Anyway. I can't wait till you move yo' ass up off Bank head and on up to Buckhead, so you can quit acting like you do. Bitch!"

Shuga saw there was no use in talking to Ray'neisha, who had flopped down on her couch and started picking at her baby toes corn through her cheap PayLess two for one sandals.

"Stank! Listen up! Here is the deal. What I need is shit for me in a size seven juniors or six in misses and Mineta size seven in little girls. Whenever you see something, I need it all. Don't just get me the shirt by itself. I want the bottoms to match, the belt, the purse, and the shoes. I want it all. Shit got to be on point. I know this card good for at least ten stacks." She lied. She did not know if the card was good at all.

"A black American Express? I thought they was green. I don't know about using this. Who you get to make this one?"

"Bitch this legit! So, gone work, ya magic!"

Ray'neisha had worked her nerves. She did not know why she fucked with her anyway, she thought, nudging her big ass out the door.

"And I don't care if it's four o'clock in the morning. Bring my shit! I'll see ya!"

***

Seven twenty-five a.m. and the phone was ringing. A wakeup call, but Shuga was already up. Ray'neisha had left no longer than an hour ago, bragging on wherever she went that the card was accepted hassle-free. Then they had chilled, talked shit, smoked a few blunts, then went through all the shit she had got them.

Shuga was hot, after the fact. She herself never got her hands dirty, but if Kresa would've answered her phone, she could've went and saw upfront what was what, cause Ray'neisha got over this time. Her whole car was loaded down but was not no way Shuga was going doing no dirt with Ray'neisha, who looked like she could not even afford shit out the Dollar Tree.

Then again, Shuga was not about to kiss Kresa's ass. She had texted her, and when she was ready to hook up, she had hit her back.   Shuga never thought twice on the possibilities that Kresa could have still been locked up.

Shuga had circled four places out of the Atlanta Journal-Constitution home rental section for her and Chris to go look at. She had it figured out already which place he would rent for her. Last night, Ray'neisha had told her how her baby brother's fifth baby momma sister Roewanda had just rented a nice house through Section 8 out in Clayton County that she had not even moved into. Shuga's mind never stopped scheming, and at three something in the morning, she called Roewanda, waking her out of her sleep to ask if she wanted to make a quick seventy-five dollars. Roewanda, who really did not trust Shuga, reluctantly agreed, only if the money was paid upfront.

"Bitch, you gotta break me off first! Cause if yo' bullshitting ass scam backfires, I 'ma have me-me!" She crooked out.

"Whatever slut!" Shuga said into the phone at the jealous seven-kid-and-another-in-the-making-hoe. "My shit tight! Stay tight! Shit'd!"

"So, what I gotta do? I just know it's some bullshit. Oohhh! I just know it is! Always is with you!"

"Is you with it or not?"

"I need the money! Hell, you know I do!"

Shuga got arrogant, "Well bitch, all you gots to do is meet me at your new house at nine-thirty and act like you showing it to me to rent."

"Act like I'm showing you my house! For what? Bitch, you ain't finna mess me up with my Section 8. You know that's a government program. Not only would I not have a place to stay for me and my kids, but I could end up landing some Fed time. N'all Boo-Boo! I'm straight! Cause what if they find out? I don't think so!" Roewanda was fully awake now.

"How they gone find out?" *'Dumb bitch! What you gone do?' Tell them?'* Shuga asked silently.

"Like the government find out about everything else- informants, and shit! They got cameras hidden everywhere!"

Shuga gave no comment on Roewanda's foolishness like the government was really gone do some extra work for her insignificant ass. "Bitch, do this, and I'll double it."

"A hundred and fifty dollars! Damn!"

"Yes, bitch. A hundred and fifty dollars and all you gotta do is show me the fucking house. It'll take five minutes, and when I get there, I'll have ya dough. Aight?"

Silence.

The silence was so long Shuga debated if she was going to have to triple her offer. She was not about to let Roewanda play her, though! But she did need this bitch, and scared money did not make money.

Then out the blue, she grunted out a, "Yeah-"

Shuga hung up before she could say more.

"Ray'neisha! Why that bitch be tripping? She don't ever want to get to the money!"

"Bitch you know she can't get locked up, not with all them kids. You know this makes her seventh."

Unmoved, Shuga rolled her eyes in disgust. "Well, it ain't like she keep them. So what's the difference?"

"True!" Ray'neisha agreed, nodding her head.

Chapter 11

Chris was there at exactly eight with breakfast in hand for both Shuga and Mineta.

Mineta took her chicken biscuit and ate it within seconds, once again, embarrassing Shuga like she had not been feeding the child. Mineta was full of questions about what kind of house they were going to get, but her excitement was soon deflated when without warning, she was dropped off at school. She then begged and begged to be included in the house hunting, but Shuga was not bulging. She did not feel like being bothered with Mineta all up in her mouth, being grown. So, Shuga utilized her babysitting service, school, because perfect attendance was never one of Mineta's requirements.

At each house, she nit-picked, making sure she found something wrong until she got to Roewanda's.

In the morning's sun, the little house with the white picket fence sat shining bright and welcoming.

"Ohhh, it's on a hill," Shuga faked excitement, thinking she would never move way out here, all in the boondocks for no shit like this. *'What the fuck was Roewanda thinking knowing she didn't even have a car.'*

If she was not hating like usual, she would have admitted it was nice, especially considering it was free. Shuga met up with Roewanda at the door and flared her nose in disgust at the sight before her that looked nothing like a homeowner, attempting to rent out their house, but like the welfare recipient, she really was.

Dressed so tacky, with rollers peeping out under a headscarf, Shuga wanted to slap her...and she would if she blew this for her.

Really alley and unprofessional, Roewanda just stood there staring.

"We is here to see the house!" Shuga said, jaded, and walked in.

"Un-huh. You know its a fee, don't you?"

"A fee to see the house?" Chris questioned doubtfully.

"No baby, she's talking about the application fee. When I called earlier, she let me know... I thought I told you that. Oh, I musta forgot."

"Well, how much is it?" Chris asked, going in his pockets.

"Two hun-"

"Twenty-five dollars." Shuga cut Roewanda off, "and I got it." "Where can I fill the application out at? The kitchen?"

"Yeah, if you got the application fee," Roewanda said, winking, continuously, like something had just flew in her eye, then penguin walked struggling to make it the few paces to the kitchen.

"I'll be right back." Shuga turned around to stop Chris, who was right on her heels following them.

"Here! Bitch!" Shuga, whispered, forcefully.

"Thank you! If I woulda knowed the big baller with the Range was in on it, I woulda charged a lil' bit mo! Ain't no telling what kinda shit you got up your sleeve!"

Shuga just ignored her and walked back to meet Chris.

"That was quick."

"Oh, it wasn't a real application. She just wanted my name and phone number for contact and a reference." He nodded. Then they looked around, and as planned, Shuga loved everything about the house.

"A thousand dollars a month for that house is good. Isn't it, baby?" Shuga asked once back in the truck.

"So, you like it? You think this is somewhere you'd wanna live?"

"It's better than where I live now, right?"

"Yes!" He said quickly, and Shuga rolled her eyes.

Then like a calculator, Shuga added up, plus spent in her head that thirteen thousand dollars that Chris was walking inside the Wells Fargo Bank to get. She knew everything she would buy.

"Do you want to get a late breakfast?" Chris asked, placing the money envelope in Shuga's lap once he hopped back in.

'Hell no!' She thought but did not dare say. She did not want to get shit with him or do shit with him now; all she wanted to do was go spurge.

"Sure, there's an IHOP a block up."

Little did he know this was it. No longer did he exist in her world. He had given her more money than she had ever seen at once, and she had gotten the big head. Shuga lived a day by day existence. Never was she the type to think about the future or put away for a rainy day. All Shuga could process was with those thirteen G's she was about to hook her shit up, get some 26's thrown on her Charger, and do some major shopping.

Halfway through the meal, Shuga's eyes bucked, and her thoughts got distorted. Cage had just walked into the restaurant with two of his boys. Cage was one of the niggas, who was getting major bread in the streets of the 'A.' Shuga had heard of him and seen him but was never able to get close to him. Here opportunity had presented itself, and she was not ready as she sat across from major lame Big (but really little), Cee!

Shuga made sure she gave him direct eye contact, so she would get noticed from the time he walked in till the time he was seated. She was sweating him hard! Too bad Cage did not glance her way, so he did not notice he had a stalker, but Chris did.

Chris frowned, following her eyes. "You know them, dudes?"

Nope, she ain't know them. Just wanted to. Shuga looked stunned at Chris, realizing she had been caught. She looked back at Cage, then at to Chris with pity in her eyes. Chris would be alright. He was a decent guy and would make some chick happy.

Shuga just was not that chick. They were on two different levels. He did not have that street creditability that she sought and longed for and thought she needed in a nigga. Whenever she stepped out with her dude, she liked for all the hoes to center their talk for the next two days on her and her man. She knew if she got with a nigga of Cage's status, she would be the next seven day talk for sure.

"Yeah. Dude use to mess with my sister. They got a kid together." The lie rolled off her tongue so easily. Shuga was unbelievable with her tactics. "I didn't even know he was back in town." She continued, with her story not missing a beat, the whole while her lust-filled eyes stayed glued following Cage's every move.

Chris caught her off guard when he said, "Well, go catch up with him."

"Huh?" Shuga jaw dropped.
"Go talk to ya' folks. Get up to speed while I make this call."

"Oh. Okay?"

By this time, Cage had realized that Shuga was sweating him. Shuga, who was never scared, stood up, and as soon as Chris was out of eyeshot, strutted like a supermodel over to the men's table.

"What up, Shawty?" One of Cage's boys hollered like she had come to talk to him. That shit pissed her off. She knew he could tell that she was the type that went for the big men with big money only!

"Aye, you need to clean yo' nose," Shuga spit with venom while pointing at the booger that was on the verge of falling out. It sucked in and out with each breath the dude took.

"Shawty, fuck you! I know I ain't got no boogers in my nose bitch!" He popped off with it still dangling.

"Ain't you that bitch from the overlook that live by Kim?" The other friend that would have been cute excepted he had his oversized '85 open-faced gold hanging out his mouth, asked.

Shuga recognized him as behind the times Ren, Cage's main man, who was stacking major bread as well. For that reason, 'only,' she smiled a very fake smile at his comment without cursing him out. The tip of her tongue burnt, from her holding back on her, telling him what he needed to go do with himself.

"Shawty, what's up?" Cage said, standing up leaning over, whispering in her ear. The man smelled so good! "I know you ain't come trying to holla at these niggas, so what's up? You trying to kick it with a nigga or what?"

Shuga was beyond turned on. "You know this," she said, hoping that Chris stayed where he was.

"That's what's up." Cage said as he openly checked her out. From her polished pink toes to her body that was banging on to her face...and hair! He loved the hair! Everything was on point. The total package was approved.

"Let's ride!" He smiled, showing her perfect grill, and Shuga's panties got wet.

Just like that, Shuga left before Chris made it back and was seated riding high in Cage's platinum, Hummer H3. Quickly, she turned her phone off cause at any minute, she knew Chris would be blowing it up.

***

Bree's emotions were overriding all of her common senses, so much so that she honestly could not see how deep Quent's love for her ran. It was so deep and real, Quent had no problem wedding her. That was in his longevity plan for their future. He even went out and got her a yellow canary six-carat platinum engagement ring.

Quent's momma had wanted a big wedding that would take months and months to plan. Shuga wanted a fly to Vegas and get married at the drive-thru chapel in ten minutes. And let 'I do' be the reason. She did not care how trashy it was; she just wanted to get it done. It did not seem the least bit tacky to her as she used Bree's tablet to surf the net to find a place. Quent and Bree decided to go to the courthouse where they eloped and later had a big reception.

A big reception where Bree showed out and showed her ass. If one didn't know, one would have thought it was a going-away party for Quent, who was on his way to fight in the war or something by the way Bree hung on his shoulder and did not want let him out of her sight.

Finally, Shuga had pulled Bree away because she was needed to take pictures. Bree would not listen to the directions of the photographer, and each picture showed Bree looking a different way, following Quent, until she turned her head for only a second and lost him. Panicking, she rushed off to find him. The cameras click caught her looking like the runaway bride. She found Quent by a group of women she did not know.

Mugging, she stomped her way over, looking ready to bust any fuck shit up.

"Who are they?" Bree all but screamed.

Quent cocked his head to the left, taken aback, semi embarrassed, he did not understand why she would come at him like that. Who did she think it would be? And invited to their reception?

Was she serious?

"These are my aunts, Carla and Deanna, and their kids... This is the love of my life. My wife, Bree." Quent introduced everyone.

Bree looked closer and realized it was two women who favored Quent's mom, and some preteen girls. If Bree's dark skin could blush, it would have been red. She played her actions off by offering a weak handshake and prayed Quent had not noticed how rude she was.

For the rest of the night, Quent tried to make it special for Bree and never left her side. He was easily in love with Bree, but because of all these her newly developed insecurities that she failed to realize, he was being pushed away.

She had become paranoid of his actions. He saw this and did not like the shit. She was losing it and in the process, was losing him as well.

More than anything, Quent hated for anybody to grill him. He was not the roody-poo type of limp dick nigga to let his bitch be all up in his business, thinking they could handle him. He liked the woman in his life to play the role as the woman and him to play his role as the man. But with Bree, she was going too far with everything. He could not make a move without her pumping him on the when's the why's, and the where's of all events in his life. Something in all their years she had never done, and he liked her for not doing. Now she was acting like a bill collector, collecting up on all the years she was not in his business.

Bree had even flipped out on every decent looking girl that worked in the club, busting they asses so hard that they figured none of her bullshit was worth it and just quit. The hoes that did not quit she fired, and then she really done it when she replaced all the pretty ones with replicas of beast or farm animals. Bree had turned his club- his baby- out. Then, she started bartending there. But that was only an excuse to keep an eye on him because she rarely wanted him out of her sight. Shit was getting serious!

"Quent!" A voice cried at his office door, interrupting his moment of peace.

"Come in." Peaches walked in, in tears.

"What's wrong now?" Quent asked, frustrated, not meaning to, but shit, he did have his own problems. He assumed either she needed a loan because her lights were about to get turned off, once again; Or her money-hungry pimp wannabe lazy ass boyfriend was beating her, once again; Or her drugged-out momma done got high and left the kids in the house and one of her neighbors who she was constantly arguing with done called DFACS(Department of Family and Children Service), on her once again.

Before Peaches could even say one word of what her problem was this time, Bree had karate kicked the door open furious.

"Bitch didn't I tell you to get the fuck out of here?" Bree screamed, not believing this trick was in her man's office. She said nothing, and like a madwoman, she ran up on Peaches before anyone knew what was about to happen, attacking her.

Quent jumped up, breaking up the fight pulling Bree little ass up off of the girl with one arm, then tossed out Peaches, who was screaming all hysterical like somebody was trying to kill her.

"What the fuck was that bitch doing up in here?" Bree asked, chest weaving up and down, but before he could answer or say one word, she went buck wild on him.

Quent was extra patient with her considering she had been through a lot. She had just lost their first baby, and the weight of her grief was taking a high toll on her. She could not seem to shake it.

***

"Quent, man, if I wanna go see fucking animals, I'd either stay at home chilling, watching the discovery channel, or I'll take a trip to the Atlanta Zoo with my kids. Shit'd Keisha ass bitching every time I come home saying I don't do shit with they bad asses anyway." Bald headed, Lou said, shaking his head.

"Nigga what is you saying?" Quent laughed.

"What I'm saying? You mean you gotta really ask? You don't know... For real? Look around! Quent man, its some beast up in here! Ain't one fine girl up in this bitch! What happened? This used to be the spot. The hot spot! Club Hot Shot home of the top-notch. Not no mo', I ain't paying no money to see they asses," Bald-headed Lou screamed, loud, hoping at least one of the dancers heard, and if they had, was bold enough to say something, cause he would Jon anyone of them out. He just could not understand why these bitches thought they could take their clothes off, not only in the daylight but to think they should get paid for it?

"As a matter of fact," he got even louder. "If they want me to watch they circus act, they better pay me!" He then jumped up dramatically, making a big scene to move his chair so that his back would be to the stage.

"I told him, man," Ross lame ass said just to be saying something.

"You ain't told me shit!" Quent snapped, looked around; his boys were not lying. But he had been so stressed out lately that he had not noticed the changes.

Bree had torn his club down, he was surprised folk still came out. He knew he would not come to see no shit like this. *Something had to be done!*

Quent figured maybe they needed a getaway. So, he got to planning, he would take her to what the travel agency had described and was calling the perfect lover's retreat.

Everything was all set, and they were ready to go. Hopefully, this would do the trick. She would relieve some of her pressures, and they would come back new.

Quent took Bree to Rio de Janeiro, Brazil, where she acted no better. He could not leave the hotel without her sneaking up behind him like the police. And when they did go somewhere together, she snapped on each and every single woman who came within ten feet of him.

By the time they got back home, Quent was too stressed beyond reasoning. When they made it to the house, he felt it was time to have a talk. He did not know how he was gone do it, nor did he know how she was going to respond. All he knew was something had to give.

"Babe," he said, as soon as he finished unpacking.

"What's up?" Bree was all smiles.

"Baby, I know you going through it and all. I'm going through it as well!"

Bree smile vanished. "What the fuck you talking about? I ain't going through shit... Are you cheating on me?"

"No! Please! That's what I'm talking about- that right there! You always think I'm out doing something. I ain't doing shit! Do you think if I wanted to fuck all these women that I woulda married you? I married you because I made a commitment to you. You don't even realize that. I think you need to seek help."

"Seek help?" That had done it. Snap, she went! "I'm not fucking crazy? I don't need no fucking help!" She screamed, out to the top of her lungs, foaming at the mouth, while racing around the room, knocking over everything she came in contact with.

Quent, head down, just walked out the door.

Chapter 12

Shuga was determined not to play herself with Cage. Unlike the mishap with Redman, she was looking to get a man out of this deal. Even though she had left with him in no type of way did she let him touch her, and he'd tried. She was beyond ready for a nigga of Cage's street cred to be hers, and she was going to do anything in her power to make it happen. It was her time to floss a nigga like Cage, him, his car, and all he came with.

Shuga had already stopped taking calls from lil' dick Chris. Still, apparently, he did not read the memo that he was dismissed and had turned into a real-life stalker, continuously ringing her phone, leaving begging messages. In her arithmetic, she had it all figured out, and the numbers tallied that she no longer needed Chris.

Why he could not realize that is what she could not figure out.

It was her fault, though, cause she knew what happened when she let wannabes taste the honey that was in between her legs.

Sunday morning, she woke up drowsy from the night before and debated about the church. Not for herself to attend to get the Word she so desperately needed, but to drop Mineta off.

She just wanted to lay in the bed all day and enjoy the quietness. She dozed off, and minutes later, she felt a touch on her back. Slowly, becoming fully awake, she realized the shit was real. Turning over, she was met with a living nightmare.

Screaming and scared, Shuga did not know what to do. "What the fuck is you doing in my house? How the fuck did you get in here?"

Before an answer could be said, Mineta, who had been standing at the door, looking at her momma like she was out of her mind, spoke, "Girl, I let

Chris in after I seen him just parked out front. I guess he taking us to look at our new house."

For the past week, all Mineta talked about was their new house, bragging to all that came in contact with her mouth. She had even gotten into a fight at school with a girl that told her that they were too poor to move into a new house, that they lived in a project with free rent, and that her momma was always trying to take somebody's daddy. So, Mineta dusted her up real quick and left the little girl with a bloody nose.

Mineta was so excited about their new house that Shuga didn't have the heart to tell her that they weren't really moving. She was waiting till Mineta either calmed down or just forgot about it.

"Un-un!" Shuga jumped across the bed opposite of where Chris was just standing.

Shuga assumed that Chris had found out about her stealing his credit card and that they were not really moving, and he came to beat her ass for that shit. So, she snatched Mineta by the shoulders, yanking her down the steps and out the front door. They jumped in her car and made sure all the doors were locked.

A few seconds later, Chris was walking out the door with a confused look on his face. "Shuga? Why are you running from me? Get out of the car! I need to talk to you!" He said forcefully.

"Look! Get away from my house!" She could not believe this nigga.

"Listen, baby, I wanna talk," Shuga turned her head and leaned down on her horn, drowning his voice out. Mineta was confused; she did not know what was going on.

"If you don't leave now, I'm going to call the police on yo' ass and have a restraining order taken out," she threatened, not knowing what else to say.

"What?" Chris looked baffled, and more than angry, he looked hurt. He could not understand why Shuga was treating him this way.

Chris had not found out about any of the dirty shit she had done, and even if he had, he would not have done any of the things that Shuga was thinking he would. He knew he truly wanted her. He liked her so much, he never thought to question any of her motives. Not that his brain could think past her these days. He was whipped. All his thoughts surrounded her. No matter what he was doing, his vision would cloud, and she had appear.

But Shuga, never knowing real, was unable to accept anything other than drama and the thuggish ways that she was used to. That was her normal, anything outside, above, around, or beyond it, she could not fathom.

Finally, after a minute with him thinking to himself about what he had done wrong and could not figure it out, with his head down, he jumped in his truck and drove off. Shuga did not believe in whooping Mineta, but this was the day she was about to get her ass tore the fuck up!

"Mineta! I can't believe you opened that door for that fucking man! Yo ass never listens!" She screamed hysterically, as she searched for something to tear Mineta's ass up with. "You never get enough of thinking you grown lil girl. You ain't nothing but six years old. Do you understand? Six! You are a child!"

Mineta had never seen Shuga like this and knew that she was about to get it. She screamed inaudibly as snot and tears both ran, afraid of a whooping more than anything. "I only opened the door cause I thought Mr. Chris was my new daddy."

"Your new daddy?" Mineta's statement caused Shuga to stiffen. After all, she had clearly misled Mineta while exposing her to drama. "Mineta! Why would you think that?"

Mineta sobbed even harder, although she had yet to been hit. "Cause Alnina say her mommy kiss her daddy and I seen you kiss Mr. Chris. So, I thought he was my new daddy."

"No, Mineta. Come here," Shuga sat back and patted her lap. Mineta shook her head no, still putting on. "Come here, baby." Slowly, Mineta tiptoed over and sat in her mom's lap, something she had not done since she had learned to walk.

Shuga could not fault nobody but herself. She had taught her nothing but shown her everything as she entered Mineta into her world.

"Listen, baby. You're a little girl, and there's a lot you don't understand, but as you get older, I'll explain. I know you didn't know any better when you opened that door...But you can't open the door for nobody anymore... none of your daddies! Nobody! Wake me up!"

Mineta nodded.

"I'm sorry for yelling at you. Are you alright?"

"Girl, I'm good!" Mineta was back all smiles.

"Mineta baby. I'm your mommy, not your girl. Call me, mommy."

"Yes, mommy," she giggled, finding that funny.

"Can you go find the phone book?"

"Yes!" Mineta jumped down and ran to get it.

Shuga located a number to Rick's lock and key service and called them out to come and install a deadbolt lock that doubled locked with a key, and that was too high for Mineta to reach.

Thank God, Shuga thought, that she did not have a back door. She could now rest assured knowing that once she locked her door, it would stay locked.

Shuga went to find her purse to fish out the bills, and as she was counting the rest of the money in her wallet, she noticed that one of her hundreds had tape on it. Upon closer inspection of the wrinkled bill, she realized it was not even a real hundred—just a one with a portion of a hundred taped in one of the corners.

"This ain't nothing, but Mark's black skinny broke ass! Fuck!" Shuga screamed, hating that cheap game playing bastard.

The real reason she was fye hot with his ass was because as many games as she played, Mark always found a way to outplay her? He just proved she was being tested and needed to step her game up. These muthafuckas was getting slick these days! And she was just gone have to get slicker!

***

After a full two weeks had passed, Kat just assumed her prison paranoia had gotten the best of her and had her thinking that Redman actually remembered who she was from all that time ago. She had eventually figured he could not have, because if he did, then LA would have already confronted her with that bullshit.

LA had not acted any different since that day; in fact, if it was possible, he had gotten sweeter.

Kat was convinced that all of those years back when she was tore up on that shit that her look of today was so stunningly different that no one would believe she was the same person from back then.

"Baby? Did you say yes or no?" LA interrupted her thoughts.

"Huh?"

"About going to Redman's lil girl birthday party tonight. His girl, Felisha, can throw a kid's party that shouldn't be for nobody but grown folks. How you gone have beer and liquor and blunts at a one-year-olds party? Shawty, some people need to get their shit together. I'm telling ya. When we have kids, they gone be respected... I bet our babies gone be cute to death."

"Yeah," Kat smiled nervously, breaking a small sweat, from just the mention of Redman's name. She wished LA would keep it strictly business with that nigga.

"So, what is it? Yea or nay?" He asked again when she did not answer.

"N'all boo, I ain't up for going to no party with people I don't know. You know that ain't my thing."

"I feel ya. I really don't wanna go either. That nigga got bout eight or nine kids, always thinking somebody wanna buy something for they bad asses. Shit'd I'm trying to make my own babies." He grabbed at her thong and pulled it down. She smiled, wiggling her body to help him free her of the skimpy piece of cloth. She grabbed his back in total bliss as his member found its way to her waiting hole. He entered her like she was made just for him.

Slowly, he moved up and down, looking in her eyes as they made love.

He kept his strokes slow, "Baby, you feel so good," he said as he felt her sweetness get wetter than it had ever got. "Damn, I love you, girl," he said, speeding up.

LA tried to hold his nut but could not. He splashed inside of her. Kat rolled on top of him, getting him right back up. She did her thing as he laid there, arms folded behind his head, watching her titties bounce up and down. She had not came once, and here he was about to come again. "Slow down. Baby, slow down." But Kat was gone; she did not hear him. She rode him faster and faster than on out until her body tensed up. On sync, they reached their sexual peak releasing together.

"Damn, I love you," he told her again.

"I love you too," she leaned down, kissing him.

***

LA and Kat laid next to each other, daydreaming in their own little worlds. Neither one wanted to leave the other. It had gotten that deep. Kat did not mind that, nor did she have anywhere to go or anything to do. Other than shopping, she had centered her life around LA. Finally, after hours of them just enjoying each other, LA eased-up stretching.

"Baby, I gotta make a run," he kissed her. "I ain't gone be gone long. You gone burn something while I'm out?"

"Ha-ha! You know that was an accident!" Kat pouted, sitting up, pulling the sheet with her covering her breast.

LA pulled the sheet back down, making Kat blush.

"N'all boo, I like burnt chicken for real!" He laughed when she did not respond; he told her he'd be back in an hour. He kissed her again, as he exited, then he dipped back around, "Make sure you look through those brochures so we can decide where you gone go."

Kat nodded eagerly. She had decided she would go to college to become a fashion designer, and LA had not laughed, but supported her and told her that he believed in her. That she could do it. LA had Kat feeling she could conquer the world.

Kat could not control her blushes as she reminisced every moment that her and LA shared. Filled with a joy she had never experienced. She never knew that having someone to love you could feel this good. She was fulfilled in every aspect and never would envision a change. For once, she was truly being loved. She went into a deeper daze at the thought of how much she deserved these feelings and the man that gave them to her.

Chapter 13

Once Chris had left, he did a rewind on his actions and repeatedly for the next twenty-four hours rung Shuga's phone nonstop. Chris had become obsessed and refused to stop calling her...

All Shuga could think was, *'Did the nigga ever sleep?'*

The only good out of it was a message Chris left claiming that he would not show up at her house unless he was invited. Well, if that was the case, he would never set foot in her domain again.

Still, something was inside of her was not trusting him not to be there when she turned around. This made her watch her every move and check twice before making that move.

The ringing would not stop, and she could not turn her phone off because she was scared of what call she might miss. The phone rung so much it was hard for her to get a call in. In between Chris calling her, she had started calling Cage. After what seemed like a hundred tries, she got ahold of him, and he was supposed to had picked her up at seven. Here it was eight minutes to eleven, and still no Cage. She had to have missed his call, seeing if she was ready for their date, because of Chris's stalking ass. She hated him even more.

Pouting up her steps, mad at being unable to get in touch with Cage, she just wrapped her hair up and was about to walk down the block to get Mineta when she heard beat vibrating through her windows.

Running to look out her window, minutes after midnight, Cage made an appearance.

Her doorbell rung as she rushed to comb her wrap back down. She slide into her Chanel sandals and ran out the door.

Cage, who looked like he was trying to walk in the house, was blocked when she slammed the door behind her.

"You acting like you don't want a nigga in yo' crib?"

"That ain't it."

"I ain't wanna go in there no way," he laughed joking but was dead-ass serious. He got paranoid when he was high and by himself.

Shuga did not care, even if it was late and a Tuesday, that this was Hot Lanta, and there had to be still plenty to do and lots of hoes that were still on the prowl that could witness her and Cage out and report on it like it was live late-breaking news. Shuga held a big goofy grin at the thought and could not wait till it got back to her circle and somebody called to ask her about rubber band popping Cage.

As good as that sounded like rap to her ears, that was not even a mini part of Cage's plan. He headed straight to the hotel. The movie that he was supposed to have taken Shuga to see earlier, *'I Can Do Bad All By Myself,'* he had taken his main girl Re-Re. Yet, he still went and picked Shuga up for his after-movie entertainment. She had called his phone all through the movie, but he had ignored her bullshit and was there now cause she had a fat ass, he wanted to hit it. That was settled after his boys had amped him up on how much of a freak she was. Shuga could tell with one look he was sloppy drunk, but that still did not stop her from cruising down I-75. She tried to make small talk, but he had one thought on his mind.

"So, what's up?" Shuga asked.

Zoned, he answered. "The sky baby, the sky," then laughed.

"So, you still be messing with Re-Re?"

"Re-Re?" He did a triple take. He knew this hoe could not be seriously questioning him about his bitch.

"Yeah. That chick you used to fuck with."

"Shawty! Whoa-whoa-whoa! Lets back the fuck outta a niggas life! Feel me? I'm with you right now, and that's all that matter... Aye, Shawty, come talk to my friend," he said, pulling out his fully erect dick, plopping it hard on the steering wheel. Sheepishly, he looked over at her. She was frowning, wondering in her head why this nigga was trying to play her.

"Watch out!" She screamed, just as she turned straight and saw that they were about to collide with another car. He had to swerve to avoid running into the back of what looked like Chris's black Range Rover.

Cage slid over to the next lane and passed the truck that was creeping in the fast lane. Shuga ducked but looked over at the truck expecting to see

Chris's yellow Chris Brown looking ass. Inside was only a white couple, and she was relieved.

"N'all, baby. You just need to watch the road," she said, to say no to his request without really saying no. Shuga wondered again, why was this nigga trying her like that?

Cage wanted Shuga's full pouty lips wrapped around his dick so bad that the thought alone had him precumming. Then he skeeted. He could not wait. They made it to the Super 8 hotel, and Shuga was pissed, not at the fact that he had taken her to a cheap dirty hotel, but about the cheap dirty hotel's location.

Cage had taken her to the boondocks of Bartow county's Redneckville! Shuga knew she would not see no one way out here. Grabbing up a brown bag off the back seat's floor and rushing inside the room, he wasted no time getting naked.

"Here," he threw her the remote. "You can order your movie now." He laughed, but Shuga did not catch that he was being facetious. Cage was under the covers and calling out to Shuga before she had finished pressing the buy button on the TV's remote.

As intoxicated as Cage was, her hesitation was apparent. "Baby... Baby, come on up here with big daddy. Shawty, you know you is too fine! Take them clothes off and let a nigga see how good you look without them. You know I'm thinking about keeping you with yo' fine ass." He sweet talked her.

And that was all the motivation Shuga needed to hear.

"Surprise! Surprise! Surprise! Look, I got some candy for you." Cage opened his hand to reveal a fist full of colorful X-pills.

"Candy? This ain't no damn candy! Crazy!" She laughed.

"Here, baby. Take you bout three or four, maybe five, and you'll never forget this night with me." She made a suspicious face. "But there'll be plenty mo! Plenty, mo!" He added. Smiling, she took five.

Seductively, Shuga did a striptease undressing. Cage's eyes stayed wide open. Even though he had said the first thing that came to his mind, he was not lying when he had popped off about Shuga being fine.

First, her round brown ass looked like it was a picture product advertisement for FYI jeans. Her breast was compliments to her small waist, which said thanks to her curvy hips. All that and she was beautiful in the face. Jiggling naturally, she made her way over to Cage. "You want baby to show daddy what really feels good?" Shuga purred out, moving the covers back. Bending face down, ass up, so high it could be seen from the front. The view Cage got off her ass looked like the top of an apple.

Looking up into Cage's eyes, she willingly took his nine inches in her mouth like a pro, taking it all the way to the base. Cage was in ecstasy as he felt her tonsils. He was in Shuga's mouth for no more than a good minute, when she felt his muscles tighten.

'I know this nigga ain't bout to come that quick?' She asked herself silently.

He was!

She frowned!

He had!

She shook her head and lifted upon just in time for his nut to splash all over titties. She rubbed it in like it was part of the master plan.

Cage must have read her thoughts because defensively, he snapped out. "The first one always comes quick!"

He had popped some 'E,' but it was not giving none of the effects it usually gave him.

Shuga, however, was extra. All that yada-yada-yada about not giving him none got played to the left once the 'E' was in effect. After he had shot off, she went back to sucking him, only he was not getting hard. His soft flesh would not bulge or stiffen. It just kept flopping side to side as she tried to pump it. Was not nothing happening.

"Here," Cage said, pushing Shuga up so 'he' could turn over on to all fours like a dog.

'What the fuck is he doing?' Shuga wondered as he cocked his head around to look at her in the position she should have been in. Shuga assumed he just wanted her to lick his balls and maybe asshole. She had not heard of a real man liking that asshole shit, but if it could help her to get where she needed to be, then so be it. She would lick them balls and that asshole.

Besides, tonight was different. Cage was that man she wanted, and she was where she wanted to be- with him, so she spread his fat juicy ass cheeks apart and placed her hot tongue on his hole, licking in long strokes. Before long, Shuga had Cage screaming like a bitch and in the bitch's position.

"You can put yo 'finger in it'," he whispered, moaning out to her.

'Huh?' She just knew she had not heard him right. Only she had because he repeated it, louder.

"Put yo 'finger in it'."

So, she did!

Maybe if she had not been under the influence of drugs, her common sense, or one of her senses, could have kicked in and made her think twice about that request.

Then again, maybe she would not have.

In her eyes, Cage was that nigga, and she had not seen a swag like his in a while.

As soon as he got her finger action, she started stroking his dick, and it sprung to life.

It had even gotten harder than when she was sucking it. Shuga was so turned on by that freaky shit that her pussy was running wet. She wanted him inside of her bad. She continued satisfying him until she was ramming not only her pointy finger but all four fingers in and out of his wide asshole. He was screaming and throwing it back.

Shuga laid on her back, but Cage flipped her on her knees and slipped his iron man in her slithery wet dripping pussy making big circles. She wanted to feel steel slamming in and out, but he only teased her, and it just made her wetter. He pulled his wet dick out that was running with her juices and poked it against her asshole. She reached back and pulled both cheeks open to allow him easy access. He sunk right in.

The 'E' had her on cloud nine, not a virgin to backdoor action, but it wasn't something she did on the first time either, but she was all into this throwing her ass back just as hard as he gave it to her. He shot a full load inside of her and was threw.

Chapter 14

Bree's actions continued to push Quent further away. Their small arguments would quickly progress into enormous fights. It was barely anything left in the eight-room house that was not broken up from Bree's fits of just spazzing out and throwing stuff.

She had not talked to her sister in a while but needed to, so she could talk some sense into her. Shuga could intercept a situation with her gift of gab and turn it around to her likings.

Too bad Bree and Shuga were two different women, with two different perceptions of life and how it should be lived. Cause Bree was losing it and did not know how to get it back. In her current state, she did not even know what the *'it'* was.

There was a strong possibility that Bree was losing her mind, but she definitely was losing her husband in this obsessed process of trying to keep him. Yet Bree did not see that; she was blind to everything that counted. It was too much. Anything that happened bad, in real life or Bree's made-up world, she blamed Quent.

Quent's thoughts of helping Bree with her depression were interrupted when his phone rung. It was Dr. Kelley, Bree's OB/GYN. Quent had called him earlier in the week to ask for a referral to a fertility specialist or to recommend a doctor for him to see because he seemed to have a problem with his sperm count.

As much as they had been trying for a baby, he had failed to impregnate Bree, and he knew that was what was wrong. Now that a child had been brought into the mix, that was what their relationship was lacking.

While Quent was explaining his problem, he sensed frustration coming from Dr. Kelley. "Quentin, there is no need to go through all of that. I don't know how many different ways I've had to explain to Bre'sha. She will 'not' be able to conceive another child."

'What?' Quent felt a blow to his stomach, but before he could vocalize any words, the doctor continued.

"I have explained to her several times that a hysterectomy is not a reversible surgery. There was nothing else we could do. She had to have the hysterectomy due to the life-threatening hemorrhaging."

'Hysterectomy?' Once again, Quent tried to speak, but the lump in his throat overpowered him.

"She's been fully educated. She knows all of this. I don't know why she insists on thinking a miracle will happen and she'll conceive a child. I've recommended a psychiatrist on several occasions. It seems you know that she's having trouble getting over this shock."

Quent was having trouble getting over this shock. He was barely able to get out a yes sir before he hung up the phone and broke down in tears.

Quent did not know who he could turn to. He could not understand why Bree felt she had to go through something like this alone. Wasn't their relationship secure enough to endure all the trials and tribulations together?

Quent did not know what to do.

He could not think.

In fact, he was not thinking when he picked up the phone and dialed his twin sister, Marqueta. He had, in one second, figured she could give him some insight on how to deal with his woman and this issue, by her being a woman. Before the end of the conversation, she had interrupted, telling him to come over, that they would finish this talk in person, acting concerned.

Only that was fake; Marqueta did not care about Bree's wellbeing, nor did she care if they stayed together or not. Because in truth, she never liked Bree. Just something about Bree did not sit well with her. Bree's attitude and the air Marqueta gave off was more than she could deal with.

Marqueta had invited Bree over to her house numerous times, and she always made excuses not to come. Bree just was not the type to sit around gossiping and wasting time. Marqueta never got the chance to know her before passing her judgment that she spread to their whole side of the family. Which, in turn, caused them not to like Bree either.

Marqueta knew from the way Quent was sighing over the phone that he was vulnerable and in need of her guidance. All that about what had been going on in his house and with his wife, Marqueta did not care. She could handle this. Pulling out her greatest trait, *'being dirty'*. She called Ashanti, a girl who used to fuck with Quent, over to her house, as well.

She was hoping to do something like a matchmaker.

Quent walked in the house without knocking.

"What's up, big bro? I didn't know you was coming over now," Marqueta lied, and both, Ashanti and Quent, saw right through her.

He did not throw her under the bus, but he was confused. He did not know why she had invited anyone over when they were supposed to be talking about his life, which was private. Marqueta felt they had done enough talking about that subject. What Quent needed was a getaway from home and looking over at Ashanti, she was fine enough to be it... if she played her cards right.

"Quent this, my girl, Ashanti. 'Shanti, this my big brother Quent... by two minutes," she added, laughing.

"Girl, I know Quent," Ashanti said, still bitter from their sexcapades that never went no further. Then when she heard that the nigga had got a wifey and wed her for real, she was hot. Marqueta sensing an attitude, but of course, she had already known the deal, had to take over this situation. Her goal was for by the end of the night to have Ashanti and Quent laid up.

Problem solved, then maybe by the end of the week, Quent could get like that boy Usher and be ready to sign them 'papers.' Laughing to herself, she decided to play the song.

"Quent, have you checked out Usher's new CD? Raymond versus Raymond?"

"N'all sis, you know I ain't into that slow shit."

"Well, you need to pick this one up. Ole boy done grew up and is speaking the truth!"

"Ohhh! I wanna hear I need a bad girl!" Ashanti shouted out like she was on the request line.

She got ignored as *'papers-papers-papers'* whispered out the surround sound speakers.

"Girl, I got some Alize. You thirsty?"

"Yeah," Ashanti said, not thinking Marqueta never offered nobody anything.

Guests do not get no drinks at Marqueta's. Guests do not get no food. They should have drunk or ate before they got to her place was her motto. She would tell ya quick, yo ass knew you was hungry for ya got here. You ain't just figured that out when you walked up in my place smelling all the goodies.

Marqueta smiled, singing loud and off-key, as she ran to the kitchen to fix the Alize that she planned to drop a mickey in it. Ashanti needed to loosen her stiff ass up, acting like she do not want a man.

Tomorrow, she would be back complaining about how she could not find one. When one in her face, she wants to act all stupid, holding grudges about shit that happened two, three, four who knows how many years ago.

She paused before reentering her living room. Only Usher's voice was heard. Dumb bitch had not even tried to spark up a conversation.

Marqueta was now thinking she should have had Nikki's freaky ass over instead.... but then again, that would not been good either. She just remembered hearing about Nikki leaving a trail of fire, and she did not want her brother walking around with unknown STD's. So, on that, she did right.

"Y'all know its a Rickey Smiley show at the Fox Theatre tonight," she strolled in.

"Yeah," Quent piped-up, thinking he had wanted to take Bree, but that turned into a no-go... "I got two tickets y'all wanna check him out?" He asked, feeling as down as he sounded.

"Yes!" Ashanti screamed. "I loves me some Rickey Smiley!"

Marqueta crooked her lip frowning. Free tickets were not that serious! Shaking her head, she said, "No, I can't make it...Why don't y'all go? You need to get out and breathe for a minute." She turned to her brother, giving him the most serious face that she could muster up.

Quent squinted an eye. *'Go out with Ashanti?'*

"It's straight with me... That's if he can," Ashanti tested Quent.

Before he could take the bait, Marqueta snatched it. She didn't want him to feel this was optional. "He a grown man, of course, he can. And that settles that."

"That's cool," Ashanti grabbed her purse.

"It don't start for two hours," Quent slowed her down. He did not know if he should do this. He had just received the biggest shock of his life, and his mind was not right.

Then again, Bree knew and purposely hid something this big from him. His angered elevated, wondering what else she was hiding?

"Why don't y'all go get something to eat? I gotta clean my house." Marqueta lied.

Quent took that as Marqueta pushing them out, cause her house stayed spotless. He was so amped up from negative energy that he was ready to go, and with all other thoughts out of his mind.

Quent took Ashanti to Strait's, a restaurant owned by Atlanta rapper, Ludacris, that served a Singaporean menu. He should have known he was wrong then, with his need to hide, by choosing a place he knew nobody he fucked with would be. Too scared to go outside of soul food. But after he ate the kung pao chicken lollipops, he wondered why he had been sleeping on Strait's.

Ashanti's company, plus the food and drinks, had put him in a mood. So, when she asked him if he wanted to skip the show and head out to her place, he was down with it.

Not once did Bree cross his mind. He was in Quent's world and had foolishly started wondering why he had never given Ashanti a real chance. He could not think of a single reason until they were finished, and instead of them just cuddling, sleeping, she wanted to talk about their future.

What future?

That was when it all came back. He knew this trick did not really believe for one second that just because he had knocked her down that they could have a title, or better yet, that this would even happen again. This was some shit he had done just because his mind was off. If he would have been clearly thinking, his love for Bree would have taken him home. With that, he ran to the shower to wash her off of him.

Marqueta heard Quent's car pulling up at her house at four a.m. She played possum as she heard him come in the house to pick up that forever ringing phone that had been left. She smiled, knowing what had kept him out till four in the morning. She couldn't wait to get the details. She once again started singing, *'ready to sign them papers-papers-papers!'*

Chapter 15

"Nigga wait a minute! Hold the fuck up! Just wait a minute! Lets back up. So, what is it exactly you is trying to say?" LA squinted his eyes in disbelief, shaking his head. *'N'all this shit can't be true.'*

"What else? It is what it is..." Redman threw his hands in the air.

"N'all dawg! I don't believe you sitting up here telling me that my girl is a trick?" LA stood up and kicked a milk crate that doubled as a coffee table at the trap. He paced, trying to catch his voice and man up from his hurt feelings that were threatening to sweep him off his feet. "N'all dawg! What I think is you got yo Kat's mixed up."

Redman sensed the hostility and could feel the emotional imbalance coming through LA's pores. The vibe he was getting, he did not like, so he decided to fall back. He could not understand why LA was taken everything he had shared with him to help him know who he was dealing with personally. This reaction was unexpected. Redman did not want no conflicts or no problems with psycho ass LA. He knew the nigga was irrational and thought psychotically. LA's demented ways were something that Redman had witnessed throughout the years. That was why Redman kept LA at bay, never wanting any beefs. Redman had not told him all that shit for what it was turning out to be. He had never seen LA with the same girl more than a few times and had originally thought Kittie would be gone by now. That she was just a fuck, like the rest of them. But LA had fooled him, sitting up here about to cry like he really cared about this slut.

"Oh yeah.... maybe," he agreed, only to get back in good graces. "Yeah, probably so, cause this girl's name was Kittie."

"Kittie? N'all, her name Kat." LA said, still looking crazy.

Redman did not like that shit; he wanted LA to know he was going out bad. That she had sold her pussy for pennies and was not no telling what she had picked up and could not get rid of. Redman was not gone tell him shit else, that was on his stupid ass.

Then thought about it. This was his boy, had been his boy since they were little niggas, he had to keep him on point. He had just give him a little something to think about, cause he knew it was the same girl. Atlanta big, but it was not that big. So, fuck it, he was gone make LA know this was the same trick. "I just remember her eyes, those cucumber eyes, and that hair. Ain't too many girls from the westside look like that. But this girl was skinny, but that was probably from all the dope, but she did have a big stupid ass."

LA did not wanna hear no more. "N'all that ain't her. My baby thick... Besides, she won't touch shit, not even that stanky green." He laughed, but not cause shit was funny. "I know she got two sisters."

"I don't know shit bout her family. We ain't kick it like that."

"Anything else you need me to clean up?" Ray J interrupted. Ray J was a local junkie that they had hired to keep shit clean.

"N'all you straight. Here," Redman handed him a fifty-piece.

Ray J almost snatched his hand off, grabbing at it.

"Nigga, maybe I do need to look around for you take that hit. I know yo' ass gone be stuck in a minute."

"N'all now! We straight. Everything good!" Ray J was babbling, saying anything to be left alone. He just wanted to be able to chill out on his flight to la-la-land. He went to his light-up area that was out the way in a corner.

"Oh! One mo' thing. I do remember this about the girl. She had a brown birthmark on her big yellow ass."

LA was stuck, feeling like he had just hit the dope that had chemicalized through the air. Without any warning, reality had snuck up from behind and smacked him hard.

Every single word of what Redman described became a movie on repeat in LA's head. His senses were on overload, allowing him to smell the stench of her derelict body. The film playing in his minds' eye was picturing her naked and near lifeless body being thrown in the empty parking lot, left for dead, not caring about the trick, laughing as they pulled away.

Fast forward, his memories, and he could see her ass in the air as he fucked her with that birthmark. He could see his tongue licking that ruined pussy that had been ran through. He spit, tasting a nasty film in his mouth that he wanted out.

"Nigga what's wrong with you?" Redman laughed nervously, sensing his big mouth had caused him some problems. Why hadn't he just shut up? "My stomach hurting." He needed to getaway. In his gut, he felt shit was not right. He would just go to the bathroom and stay till LA left. That nigga was on some trip shit, and he ain't want no part of it.

LA had flipped out like he had been shot with a dose of schizophrenia. In his world, all were against him, and Redman's words had been to taunt him, and now he was standing over there gloating.

In what seemed like a digital movie stuck playing the same image, LA loaded off into Redman.

Still, pulling the trigger long after the bullets had expired.

That front row unexpected action had caused Ray J's high to be instantly blown. His drug mind interrupting reason. He did not know whether to stay or run. His drug mind interrupting reason, telling him he was safe. Just act like he ain't see the shit he was looking right at. Once LA got through with Redman, he would be able to go through his pockets and get his dope and money off of him. Plus, he might be able to bust that lock on the basement's door. He had been trying to find a way to check that out. It had to be something of value down there. That was if LA was not planning on doing first. He did not know what was happening; all he knew was LA was far from right bright. He had not even noticed he was out of bullets.

While Ray J waited, he tried to think. He could not figure out why LA had shot Redman. What had happened that quick? Had they been arguing? He did not think so. They were just talking and laughing. Everything was all good a minute ago. He guessed it was a minute ago. Truly, he did not know how long he had been stuck. It could have been hours.

LA was still pulling the trigger, the clanking of the gun sounding off, with a sinister look on his face. Ray J choose to play his role to the T. No one took him at being anything more than a dope fiend, and he was okay with that description being set for the record. He stayed in his little light-up corner; zombie stuck like he had not heard them loud ass gunshots. Or that he had not saw how Redman's body had twisted with the force of each bullet. And how he had grabbed at LA's arm trying to steady himself with an unbelievable ghastly expression of death piercing through his eyes before he fell to the floor.

Ray J had always been told a person will take their last shit at death but had not believed it until he smelled it with his own nose. *That shit was strong too!*

Eventually, LA lowered the gun. For a moment, a look of remorse plagued LA's face. But then LA spit kicked and stomped at Redman's head until it was caved in.

Redman knew not to fuck with anything LA loved, even if it was before he loved it. Some shit people should keep to themselves. Redman should have taken that shit to the grave cause he still took that shit to the grave.

LA stepped his bloody timberland boot out of Redman's head and looked over at Ray J, who had his eyes crossed and mouth twisted. He tried to make the face he had been told about when he got high. LA went in his pocket and pulled out a thick wad of money. He did not count it, just threw the bundle to Ray J.

"Clean this shit up!"

Ray J looked at the money and felt he had been blessed. He now knew the meaning of being in the right place at the right time. Pam, his ole lady, would let him back in the house now he could pay her back for that TV he had stolen from her and pawned last week.

LA, walked out leaving a bloody boot trail behind him.

Chapter 16

'Seven whole days and not a word from you,' Shuga sung alone with Toni, but she could not have been feeling her, because she was not on her way.

A whole week had gone by, and Cage still had not returned any of Shuga's calls after that night they'd shared that she felt was magical.

Once again, the hot girl realized, too late, that she'd played herself.

She should have had that one figured out sooner, instead of wasting a week of wishing, when she had woke up early that next morning alone.

Luckily, she had carried her purse cause if she had not, she would have been on stuck. Cage had just up and left.

Silly Shuga had waited, making up excuses for Cage's actions, telling herself he had made a business errand and would be back in time to do brunch. But that never happened. In the end, she was mad and embarrassed that she had to ride home in a fucking cab. She knew her nosey ass neighbor Kim was somewhere lurking and taking notes. Now everybody was gone know she had been stranded out in Bartow County to be pulling up in a Red Bird cab. And just to think all that night, she was for sure that she would have him whipped by the time morning came.

"No, James! No James! No James! Somebody help me! Anybody! Help! Please! Please!"

Shuga's own pity party was interrupted when her ears were filled with Shawan screaming to the top of her lungs

"Shuga! Girl! Damn! James is out there beating on Shawan's stupid self," Mineta ran in to inform.

Shuga, so deeply depressed, did not have the energy to check Mineta for cursing.

She only went to the porch when Mineta started screaming for Shawan and James to get their asses away from their new car.

"Oh, fuck no! Mineta, go get my keys. I'm bout to move my damn car. Out of all these raggedy-ass cars parked out here, they wanna run they asses around the best shit out here. Come on, Mineta, and put yo' shoes on."

"They is." She said, running with not only Shuga's keys but her purse too.

Shuga strutted, fussing right to her car where Shawan was posted at her hood, while James was at the trunk trying to ease his way around.

"Hit his ass for me, girl! Please-please-please hit his ass!" Shawan begged.

"No bitch! You hit his ass! Yo' dumb the one that keep letting his no good, sorry, lazy ass back in!"

"Not no more! I promise! This it! Help me! Help me! Help me! Please!"

Shuga opened her door, ignoring Shawan's pleas letting Mineta climb through the driver's side. If James, doped out ass was still behind her car when she put it in reverse, that was gonna be on him. As soon as Shuga put the car in gear, Shawan tried to make a run for it but was too slow. James tackled her to the pavement, stomping at her head and stomach like she was his worst enemy and not the mother of his kids, as their babies stood in the doorway watching helplessly and crying.

"You wanna go over, auntie Kresa?"

"Do I? Why no! You know her house be all nasty with stuff everywhere...So no! No, I don't!"

"Well, we going and don't say none of that when we get over there, okay?"

"Whatever," Mineta snapped, then added, "I don't know why you asked me like I had a choice. You should've just kept that to yourself. Now I gotta know where we going and think about it the whole time. At least I could've thought we were going somewhere good! Huh!"

"Shut up!" Shuga screamed but was not heard because Mineta kept right on going with her smart comment and complaints.

"Kresa, open the door. I'm pulling up," Shuga phoned her.

"Open my door for what?" Kresa responded with an attitude.

"What do you mean for what? I done drove all the way crosstown. What you got company or something?"

Kresa sucked her teeth. "Nope! I just don't feel like being bothered with nobody." Before Shuga could respond, Kresa was snapping. "Bitch, when I was locked up, was you around? Now all of a sudden, I'm out, and you wanna show face. Ain't nothing!"

"Kresa, what are you talking about?" Shuga had gotten so involved in her own life that she had not bothered, thought, or even cared to check on Kresa.

"What do you mean, what am I talking about? Like you didn't know!"

"Bitch open the door!"

"I said, I don't want to be bothered."

"Bitch, open the door," Shuga screams, ending the call.

Mineta's fingers were crossed, and she started praying that Kresa did not open the door.

"Gas is damn near five dollars a gallon ain't no way I done waste almost a half of tank," Shuga said, talking to herself.

Mineta was just about to tell her she'd give her the gas money back if they could just go home, but Shuga had rushed out the car. When she got to the door, Kresa was standing blocking her way, looking nappy-headed.

"Bitch, what's up with your head? And why is you so fucking big? Are you pregnant?"

"N'all hoe! This county weight."

"County?"

"Yeah, the fucking county jail! I just got out a few days ago. Don't act like you didn't know."

"I didn't."

"So you mean to tell me you ain't get none of them messages for me?"

"About a month ago, I got one... but I thought you had bond out."

"N'all," Kresa huffed. "Ain't nobody bail me out. I went to court and got put on probation. But anyway, what is it you want?"

"Kresa, chill with the attitude, cause I didn't know. It's not like you tried to call back."

"I shouldn't have had to call back. I called you once. Your boy didn't tell you what the fake ass rapper did to me?"

"My boy?"

"Yeah, that ole fake ass pretty boy you was with that night."

"Bitch, I don't fuck with his lame-ass!"

"Good! Cause they flexed up as fuck!" Kresa screamed out, still mad. "I had got arrested for assault on the police."

"For real?"

"Yes! Me and that lame ass nursery school rapper had it out! At first, we was chilling, smoking blunt after blunt, then all of a sudden, this nigga pulls out a crack pipe!" Kresa lied.

"What?" Shuga was in shock.

"Yes, bitch! You know I ain't with that shit."

"I feel ya! That shit turned my sister out! I know what it'll do!"

"Bitch, that nigga musta thought he was gone turn me out like I was some simple-minded groupie that was gone fall over his every word, cause of who he think he is. I wouldn't do that shit regardless. That nigga was trying to act millionaire status but couldn't even throw a bitch a dollar. Then the nigga called his self-wanting to fuck after he done beamed up to Scotty. I was bout to come get you, but I didn't want yo' dude to think I was hating. Anyway, the nigga said he wanted to eat me out."

"For real?" Shuga was wide-eyed, listening intensely to this make-believe.

"Yeah, girl, so I busted on the niggas face. What the hell? I knew what it was, but I played his game. He thought after he ate me, I was gone be down with it. Not! Nigga ain't playing me! I played his ass. As soon as I bust on his chin, I put my clothes back on. And that's when me and nigga got into it. He really thought I was gone fuck his two-inch dick ass?"

"Bitch you don't say! Two-inch dick?"

"Yes!"

"So was his partna!" They both laughed, and Kresa wondered if Shuga was lying on ole boys dick like she was.

"Yeah, bitch I had to call security on his ass, just so I could get the fuck out the door. Then when they got there, he gone flip the script. I guess cause he was embarrassed and shit, talking bout he wanted me out. Yeah right! Then didn't wanna give me my purse, so I spazzed out on his ass. I needs my shit! That's when the police grabbed me, and I went ballistic on they ass too! Like they couldn't get none." Kresa felt good with telling this version, passing it off the truth.

"Bitch, that nigga was Looney fucking Tunes, ya heard!"

"And bitch, the thing is I had read in one of those tabloids that he was out there and had did times in a mental institution. But I didn't want to believe it."

"How the hell we get caught up with them, lames?"

"Bitch, I tried to tell yo ass! I tried to! I had told you from the jump we should have found us some real ballers," Kresa pointed her finger. "None of this would've happened."

"Damn, I ain't know, cause ole boy had started stalking me." Shuga then filled Kresa in with all the details of the escapades she'd missed. "Still, you should have called me back!"

"I didn't know. Anyway, I had some time to think and put some shit into perspective, and that shit I had done to Eric as was payback. Karma is that bitch. That bitch don't knock; she just busted in. She coming whether you want her to or not. That shit had me sitting lonely for forty days and forty nights."

Kresa put her head down like a sick puppy, and Shuga didn't want to keep this pity party up.

"Speaking of payback. This is what I came to tell you. Did you on know that nigga Redman got killed at his trap?"

"Hell n'all."

"They say it was a robbery, cause wasn't no money or dope found nowhere."

"That's fucked up! These niggas is dropping like flies!"

"His wake tomorrow. You gone go pay yo' respect?"

"I ain't paying nothing," Kresa laughed. "But I 'ma go. Ain't no telling who gone be up in there! I wonder if him and Eric knew each other?"

"I don't know. Have you talked to Eric since you been out?"

"No, but I did try to call him a couple times. He don't never answer, though. You ain't seen him out and about?"

"Nope. Come to think about it. That nigga been MIA since that night. I ain't seen him or Erica."

Kresa blew a hard breath. "I didn't ask if you'd saw that bitch. How many times am I gone have to tell you I don't give a fuck about that miscellaneous trick! Especially now! I'm so focused!"

"Whatever! Kresa, he's probably still salty about that night, and don't want to talk to you."

"I don't know. That shit so old." Kresa pouted. "You got your phone with you?"

"Yeah." Shuga waved it in her hand.

"Do this. Call him so you can talk for me, and I can listen and see where his head at. Ya, feel me?"

"Aight. Dial the number." Shuga tossed her the phone.

"Damn, bitch, he won't pick up from yo' number either. It's his voice mail." After a minute, Kresa asked for Shuga's phone again.

"Shuga! Help! Help! Help!" Mineta screamed, stomping around. She had been listening and had gotten an earful, and now that the conversation was dead and with that smell, she couldn't take no more.

"Girl, what is wrong with yo' as?"

"Help!" Mineta sucked in and out, blowing with her mouth while holding her nose. "I...I...I... can't breathe... Fresh air!"

Shuga grabbed Mineta's underarm and pinched it. "Didn't I tell yo' lil as not to start that shit?" she whispered. "Kresa, I left Mineta's asthma pump. Bitch I gotta go."

Once they were out the door, Shuga handed Mineta her pump and asked her why she had done that.

"I tried to hold my breath for as long as I could, but I couldn't hold out no longer. I was bout to die. It smelled like hot rotten fish in there. She should have had the air on or at least opened a window. It was just hot and stank. That smell probably on us, and people gone think we nasty."

"Mineta, we gone ride with our windows down to blow off the funk."

"Why do she smell all stank?"

"I don't know, baby. I don't know."

"But, you smelled it?"

"But I don't know, though," Shuga said, thinking back to the time Kresa had told her that she had gotten a tampon stuck up in her during sex and forgot. For about two months, she walked around with that thing in her before she noticed anything was wrong, and by that time, it had rotted and caused all kinds of bacterial infections.

Chapter 17

Kat had not expected to see Shuga, who was shocked to see Bree. Then when everyone spotted each other, they all wondered what they were doing here.

"Bitch, how did you know Redman?" Shuga asked suspiciously to Kat, who had been dragged out by LA.

Kat had made every excuse she could think of not to go, but LA insisted he needed her that she was his support. *'If she only knew.'* His best dude had been gunned down, and he could not make it by himself. *'Oh, boy, could he not!'*

LA, who had no choice but to go after Redman's mom, had designated him a pallbearer without asking. He had wanted to tell her, no, but there was no way he could. He had grown up with Redman, his mom had fed him just as much as his own. He hated that he had to go through this ordeal of burying her baby... but that was life. We live to die.

With that attitude, LA shrugged everything off. Fuck it! All that now mattered to him in life was Kat. With her, he did not need anybody else.

"I didn't know him! LA did. They were best boys or something," she barely moved her mouth, not wanting to answer Shuga.

"Umm, let's get a good seat," Shug walked to the second-row pew right behind the family.

"A good seat? At a funeral, Shuga?" Bree made it clear that she was talking to Shuga only and not Kat.

Now, Kat was so high and mighty that she didn't pay Bree's immature comments any attention. She searched around and spotted LA sitting with an old lady who was crying on his shoulder. He gave her his crooked lip smile, and then he turned back straight.

The funeral was dragging by slowly, until the preacher asked, "Would anyone like to say a few words on the dearly departed?"

All was silent, then loudly, "I sure muthafuckin' would!" was screamed by a girl who didn't look any older than fifteen, maybe sixteen. She jumped up from the back and strutted up the church's aisle in her baby powder pink Sean John bubble suit with a little boy tagging behind her.

"Com' on man-man," the girl said, rotating her neck. "All I wanna say is that Redman wasn't shit! He ain't never do shit for our son. He ain't never even bought his baby no pampers."

"Fo' real girl!" was screamed out anonymously, but Shuga knew that voice. It was Kresa's ass somewhere in the mix being messy.

"N'all, he ain't never do shit for our son, and now he dead and can't ever do shit for him!"

An elderly usher, the only one with some sense, remembered where they were and knew that this was not the time, nor the place. He attempted to pull her to the side, but he was too old, and she was too angry, so she wasn't going nowhere.

"N'all fuck that! Y'all trying to bury him in all this muthfuckin' jewelry and shit!" She screamed, pushing the old man down. She ran to the casket, snatched Redman's dead fish feeling hand, relieved him of his rings, snatched his Jesus piece, and just as she was going for the watch, Redman's sister and main baby momma ran up to intervene.

"Fuck, no bitch! It ain't about to go down like this!"

"Stupid bitch! He ain't do shit for that lil bastard cuz he knew it wasn't his," Redman's sister screamed.

Then they double-teamed young baby momma. Licks were being thrown from every direction.

"Bitch look at these hoes!" Kresa had come up from behind laughing. "So, you, Kitty Kat?" Kresa asked like she knew all about her. Before Kat could confirm or deny, she was all in her business, questioning her on if her and LA were really together, but not waiting for an answer. "Cuz bitch I heard he be fuckin wit Rio."

"Rio?"

"Yeah," but before Kresa could finish her report, she had belly dived to the floor.

Young baby momma had dropped some of the jewelry that she had strong-armed, and Kresa was on it. Shuga watched laughing as she slipped out unnoticed with Kat waiting and wanting to know who the fuck Rio was.

"Who is Rio?" Kat asked Shuga.

"I don't know!" Shuga responded with attitude. "Kresa, be hatin!"

"Oh?" Kat said, assuming that to be true. These days she had a lot of haters and never gave it another thought to be more than that. And when she walked out, her head was held so high one would have thought she had never been taught to look down.

***

"Cage, I'm out here where you told me to be, and I don't see your car nowhere," Shuga singsong, excited that Cage had finally decided to hit her back after weeks of hearing nothing from him.

"Bitch, you don't know every car I own and believe me, I owns plenty. Bitches'll never be able to keep up with me."

"What?" Shuga laughed, trying to save face like she had not really understood his disrespectful ass.

"Nothing." He laughed at her. "I see you finna pull up on me now. Park and walk over here with yo sexy fat ass. You see me now?"

"Yeah?"

Shuga parked her car opposite of the street, just so that she could be seen walking across the it to meet him. Cage was in a cream pearlized Lincoln MKT Crossover, still with the dealer tags in the window. Shuga had not never seen one of those.

"What's up?" He asked as she approached, exaggerating her walk.

"You know I'm trying to get with you.... tonight."

Shuga was all smiles, up until he added the tonight. He had directly let her know what was up, yet Shuga would not perceive that.

She could not see that.

She wanted to play herself.

She wanted to think that this was the man that was about to give her his all. In her make-believe world, that was what was about to happen. He pulled her closer as he groped her on her big ass.

"Whoooo!" He screamed, sliding his hand down the back of her jeans. "Yeah, big daddy needs his girl!"

"Yo, Cage! Nigga is you ready?" One of his boys ran out of the house he was parked in front of.

"Nigga, I been waiting on you. Hold up a minute. Don't you see me talking to a lady?"

"Nigga you doing it like that? What's up? Shawty?" Dude walked over to a cheesing Shuga. "Wait a minute, ain't you that trick bitch from Atlanta overlook?"

Shuga's face dropped.

'Damn!' Did everybody know her as that?

"N'all, Cage, we ain't finna waste another second on no hoe like this. We gots money to make! Money over bitches! All-day every day!" He laughed, jumping in the front of Cage's clean ass Lincoln.

Cage leaned over, licking Shuga's ear, then whispered to her that he'd see her later that night. He patted her on her ass then sent her on her way. Cage jumped in his Lincoln and sped out, not waiting to see if she made it back across the street to her car or not in this rough ass neighborhood.

When she got to her car, inside her phone was singing. Rushing to get it, she smudged one of her acrylic nails that was just done hours earlier.

"Shit!" Shuga screamed, still anxious to get to the phone. "Hey," she purred to who she thought was Cage.

"Hey yourself."

Shit faced, cause it was not Cage.

"Who is this?" She had a major attitude.

"Baby, please don't be like that. I need to talk to you. Please," he begged.

It was Chris's stalking ass. She thought he would bought the hint that she just wasn't fucking with him like that.

"Listen, you psychotic bastard," Shuga screamed so loud she hurt her throat. "What is it you don't understand? I. Don't. Want. You! I got somebody!" She lied. "This number getting changed tomorrow, so call all you want tonight bitch!" She hung up on him.

LA normally was good at honoring the position he had bestowed upon himself as playing God. Whenever he took a life, he could not even five minutes later be partying like he had not done a damn thing.

But killing Redman had strained him to the max. He never thought Redman would cross him like that. In his eyes, he had believed his money, his dope, and his girl was safe in Redman's care.

LA was looking at the situation from an unbalanced perspective like he had clearly been violated. He could never talk to anyone about what happened, and mentioning anything to Kat of what had been said could never be done because then he would have to tell what he'd done to fix it. He wished things would play out and go back to normal, but to no avail was that happening. And even though no one else knew... *He did.* And every time he looked at Kat, the events of that fateful night replayed in his head.

Ms. Reatha, Redman's mom, kept calling him, stressing him like he could bring Redman back. Even though he 'played' God, LA could not preform no miracles like that and make a nigga rise from the dead no matter how hard he tried.

Weeks later and the murder was still fresh, in his memory bank like it had just happened earlier that day. It just would not leave his mind. He should not have went to that funeral, causing that memory to be forever etched to his membrane: Redman laid in that bed of death looking well... dead, with all that dark ass markup and a suit. Redman ain't never wear no suit.

LA tried his best to act the same around Kat but was coming off as fake. He would not touch her. He just could not find himself doing nothing physical with her.

Couldn't!

It did not feel right!

Wouldn't!

Kat noticed no changes whatsoever. Her head was blown up from all the pampered princess treatment that became her lifestyle.

LA just knew Redman had mistaken Kat until he had spoken of her discolored brown birthmark. Then he knew it was the truth. This shit was too much.

"Hey baby," Kat said cheerfully, interrupting his shower, letting herself in without an invitation. He sighed heavily, but she was so lost in her own world that she did not pay any attention to his expression. He did not want to see her ass naked. She tried to hug him, but he ducked it like a football play.

"Nall, I'm rushing, I gotta make a run. I get at cha when I get back. Aight Kittie," LA said deliberately, then stepped out with his eyes glued to her birthmark.

When he said Kittie, Kat did not notice what he had called her. She was out of the shower drying off when it hit her that he had called her Kittie. Still, she brushed it off as maybe he had given her a pet nickname, turning Kat into Kittie. A lot of people would.

LA had her on a throne so high in the last few months that she was feeling herself. Her self-esteem was up there, and a new level was so high that she had mentally blocked out who she used to be.

In her mind, no longer did her former self exist. Her head was in the clouds. She had even started ignoring her sister Shuga's calls. She had felt she should cut all tries to *'that life'* that used to live. Because that was not her. She was really a new person in every aspect of the meaning. So, her new life would not include people who could bring up her old one. She felt as long as LA was in her world, supporting her that she did not need another soul. Where were they when she was lost and needed them? They were not around. So now she was found they were not going to be around her, trying to bring her down.

Bree, she did not have to worry about her. She would never call Kat. She did not fool with Kat on that level, and Kat was glad. One less person she has to deal with. To Kat, Bree thought she was better than everybody. So, *'fuck her'* was Kat's attitude.

But Shuga.... oh my God! She would not let a bitch breathe. She had called and called, leaving message after message, actually showing real concern—something she had never done. So Kat took her realness as phony made up nosiness.

Kat did not care about none of them. She was living the life she assumed they all wanted. And she did not need nobody hating around her.

"Where the fuck is it?" She heard LA screaming as she dried her body down. She started rushing to get to his aid. "Where the fuck is my shit?" He was screaming like a madman.

"Huh? Baby? What are you lookin for, baby?" She asked, rushing to where he was.

LA was in the den, frustrated, in a praying position, mumbling to himself. But she couldn't make out what he was saying.

Calmly, he looked over with bloodstained eyes and said, "I'm gone ask you once. OK. Only once. So..."

LA's soul had been turned and twisted. He did not know what to believe. He had gotten very untrusting of Kat since he had been told the news of her past. In fact, that was the only thing he was sure of that he *'would not'* put his trust in her.

He checked, double-checked his shit on the regular. Just waiting for her to slip up while trying to catch him slipping. If she was on that shit, he was gone catch it. Cause shit like that could only be hidden for long. Now he was upset at the realization that he had caught her, and it was true. He had wanted so bad for it not to be.

What LA was screaming about was a small brown bag that was missing that had been left by mistake in the table the night before. Inside the bag was a key of dope.

"What shit?" Kat chuckled nervously.

This bitch was sitting up there lying to his face. A black shadow crossed him as she stared at her, not wanting to believe the truth.

For the first time in his life, he had given his heart to a female. Even though it had been embedded from his own grains of survival tactics to never try their kind.

Why would he?

Not when his own mother abandoned him and left him for dead. Before he even knew what life was. If your own mother is not trustworthy, what woman is?

Suddenly, in one swift stunt, LA had jumped up and knocked Kat to the ground. "Bitch you getting high?" He should have known before this, from the way she was always hyper, sweating, and had started losing weight over the last few weeks. Kat could not respond because of the pain from the punches, kicks, stomps that were being administered to her body.

LA's initial attraction to Kat, unknown to all, was for the same reason he hated her life with a heated, forceful passion. That day all these months back, when he first saw he standing on that corner, he had been mesmerized. It was like he had taken a photo from a past memory and brought it to life.

LA was in love with Kat in a sick, twisted type of way. He looked at loving her as loving his mother. For Kat bore good resemblances to his high yellow, green-eyed, redhead mother. In fact, pressing rewind, ten years before she died, Kat was her; every feature was the same.

For moments when he was punching her, kicking her, and stomping her, it was not her. He was back in time knocking his mom out, trying to beat some sense into her for all the times she had turned a blind eye to the abuse her boyfriends' gave him. LA felt that deep down, she always knew but failed to protect him for her own selfish reasons. All because a few needs were met. On her death bed, he opened up and cleansed his soul of all that had happened. He thought a heavyweight would be taken off his shoulders.... but she had called him a liar.

Those flashbacks caused LA to beat Kat until she was balled up semiconscious. He spat at her, then walked out of the house, feeling physically sick.

***

Shuga convinced Kresa to go out with her by fabricating a story about hearing Eric had been spotted at Body Tap. A strip club, which in fact, Cage was known to frequent.

"Even if Eric ain't there. It's niggas with gwap that be up through there." Kresa had said, still hyped.

'I know,' almost popped out of Shuga's mouth. Luckily, she caught herself. Playing dumb, she said, "Oh, forreal? I wonder why I didn't know this."

"Yo ass probably did," Kresa said, then laughed.

"Bitch, is that Eric's M.C. with that candy shit on it?" Shuga lied, wanting to pump Kresa up because she knew that the fly ass Monte Carlo that was in view was not Eric's dusty shit.

"Where? Where?" She leaned up and started bopping her neck like a chicken.

"Right there!" Shuga pointed.

"Oh, n'all. That's Skittles, he got the Starburst logo."

"Starburst? Oh. OK," Shuga was so fake.

"But look right there bitch! That's one of them paid men I was talking bout right there! His name is Cage, and he is too fine! He be with a fine ass nigga name Ren, too. Both of them niggas as getting money. Let's go over there, while he by his self and ain't no hoe's sweating him. I'll hook you up with his friend, Ren," Kresa said to mouth, hanging Shuga and jump out the car big stomach, looking five months pregnant. She needed to go take a good shit or detox her body. She looked a hot mess, with her nappy hair in an attempted gelled down slick backside ponytail.

"Come on bitch! For he go inside!"

Shuga was stuck. There was no way she was about to let Kresa run over to Cage. She did not think for one minute he would fuck with her, but she could not be sure. His main girl, as said in the streets, looked butch, so she really could not say what his type was.

Shuga thought quickly, using her wit, she knew exactly how to handle this one. She slowly twisted over in Cage's direction while Kresa speed raced, not watching where she was said going and almost got bumped by a car as she tried to get to him first. A chorus of laughter erupted, but she didn't care. Kresa was plain tacky. By the time Shuga approached them, Kresa was running her mouth.

"Cage?" Shuga fake surprised. "I didn't 'know' this was the Cage you was talking about."

Cage looked funny.

"Hey, boo!" Shuga strolled right up to him, not caring who was around or who was looking as she took full claim, to her man-in-her-mind, and kissed him in the mouth, tongue, and all.

'You know him?' Kresa asked, dumbfounded, and without waiting for an answer, she stomped off. "You so full of shit!"

Shuga did not care. She stood there, soaking up all the attention that Cage was giving her until they were interrupted.

"I'm just out here looking for the number one sex," The unknown dude from earlier walked up singing R. Kelly, but stopped when he saw Shuga. "Cage, nigga, I know you ain't wasting time with this hoe again?"

"I ain't cha hoe!" Shuga snapped. *'Why don't he go the fuck on? Ole non getting pussy ass nigga.'* She thought.

"Damn Skippy! You'll never be shit to me. But to my boy, you might be a little suckey-suckey and fucky-fucky. Tell that bitch that we just our here looking for the number one sex. Ain't that right? MOB!" He screamed.

"Nigga fuck you! Lame ass! You just mad you can't get it!"

"N'all bitch, I told you, I don't want it!"

"You's a old sideline wanna be. Living ya life through somebody else's such a simple negro."

"Bitch!" Unknown dude screamed while shaking up his brown-bagged bottle of Corona. "What you got to say now?" He asked, laughing as he dashed Shuga's freshly permed hair with the beer.

"Hell fuck n'all, nigga," Shuga screamed, with the beer flying all in her hair, mouth, and eyes.

"What you gone do bitch!"

"T.L.! Chill the fuck out, nigga! Baby?" Cage grabbed Shuga around the waist as she tried to run up on the nigga she now knew as T.L., as he laughed in her face finding the whole thing amusing. "Wait a minute! Wait a minute! Baby! Baby!" Cage pushed Shuga back to her car. "Baby chill." He opened her door and stuffed her inside.

"N'all nigga! That nigga done fucked up. I don't know who he trying to play."

"That nigga drunk. Listen, babe. Here." He pulled out two hundred. "Gone get your hair redid, and I'm holla cha."

***

Shuga waited up and did not get that call from Cage until two-twenty in the morning. She could tell he was wasted, but she still let him come over.

As soon as she opened the door, Cage rushed in with a big ass dude behind him. "Baby," he grabbed her ass, pulling her towards him while stuffing his dry tongue in her mouth.

"Aye, my nigga gone chill here while we handle business," He told her, and she looked over at dude who had propped his feet upon on her coffee table and had snatched up her remote and was scanning the cable change pay-per-view movie guide.

No, he was not about to order, no movie.

Shuga opened her mouth, but Cage stuck that cotton tongue in her mouth again. Then he pushed her up the steps to her bedroom.

"Here," he handed her five ecstasy pills and a bottle of Hennessey, while he took eight. He had already taken seven or eight that day, maybe nine. He did not really know. What he knew was his dick was rock hard. Like a wild beast, he ripped Shuga's bra and thong off and was at her.

The 'E' was in full effect, and she was throwing everything at him. She was so into the fuck that she did not notice Cage's boy walking in the room butt naked. Cage bent her over on all fours, then he and his partna tag teamed her.

Chapter 18

Lost, LA cruised around the city with no destination in mind, just traveling to where his car carried him. Hours later, he found himself, without meaning to, in front of Rio's house contemplating, should he just go back home?

Choices.

There, LA stood knocking on Rio's door, at three in the morning. Arrogantly, feeling like it was a known fact that she was all alone and waiting for him. LA summed it up that it did not matter if she did have company, the nigga was gone have to go, bottom line.

Clearly, he was not thinking.

"Papi...qu sorprender! Papi," Rio said, heavy accented, then spoke seductively, again something in Spanish that LA didn't understand. She had come to the door, looking fresh, like she had been doing exactly what he was thinking, waiting on him. Clad in a sequin nightgown that went perfectly with her bronze skin and dazzling long jet-black hair. "Come on in Papi. What is wrong?" She asked while taking his hand, leading him straight to her bedroom. "Papi, what's wrong? You didn't call? Not that you had to. It's just you have never done this. So, I know something's up. What happened? Something's wrong- I know it! Talk to me."

"Let's not talk," he said, quieting her. While removing his shirt, he realized his hands were caked with dried blood.

Watching as Kat's blood run down the drain, and as it so did the strong feelings, he had for her.

Gone, and for what?

A hit?

Some dope?

A high?

In all of the months they had been together, he had never once thought of cheating on her, but now he looked at it as they were no longer as one. So, he went back to his 'ole ways,' ways she had kept him from with no regret. When he walked naked in her bedroom, Rio had removed the nightgown and was clad only in her skin tone colored bra and g-string, with big sexy hair floating.

She looked right in his eyes.

She forcefully pushed him to the bed and began licking his body. She knew exactly what he needed and was going to give it to him. Starting with the back of his neck, she began sucking his earlobe, following an invisible path leading with her tongue down his back she went while massaging him with her soft but strong hands along the way. When she got to his ass, she spread his cheeks apart and, with her long lizard tongue, went at his waiting hole. Sensitive shocks excited throughout LA's body. She massaged his balls as her tongue continued to merge in and out. Rubbing his rock hard dick, she played with the sticky stuff it leaked. LA flipped Rio over, taking her doggy style on all four. He needed her now, and without any protection, he entered her warm hole swiftly. She moaned in excitement, throwing it back at him. It felt so good. In minutes he was exploding inside of her. He fell back and relaxed on the bed. Rio went to wash, and by the time she came back with his rag, he was dead to the world. Still, she washed him, then snuggled up under his arm and held him the rest of the night while thinking it's about time her man came home to her where he belonged.

The next day LA woke up groggy with a serious hangover, not remembering shit until he looked at the light attempting to sliver through the black blinds. The light hit his eyes shining in on him- then in him, so hard it was like a Mack truck. He jumped straight up and could not believe that he had slept over

'Rio's.'

"*Oh shit!*" He had to get the fuck out of dodge before anyone saw his ass.

"Papi, I cooked you breakfast," She sung too cheery for him while holding a big plate of every type of breakfast food she had in the house.

"N'all. I gotta go," He said, looking around for his clothes. Getting upset. "Where my shit at?" He asked.

Disappointed, she said, "Oh, your clothes had blood on them. So, when I picked them up off the floor this morning, I soaked them, but they are in the dryer now."

"Aight- aight! I need my shit! Go check um and see if they dry."

Head down, she walked back in the bedroom with the half-dry clothes feeling confused.

The morning after...

What was happening?

She had envisioned something different for this time around.

"They almost dry."

"Yeah. Thank you." He said and could not even look at her.

"Your welcome, baby." She wanted to say so much more to make him understand what they could have, the life that could live. But did not because she knew upfront the anger streak that lived inside of LA.

So, she let him be, for now, not wanting to deal with any of that. Slowly, she could tell he was coming around, and when he did, he would be there.

When he opened the door, the bright morning sun was like a spotlight putting him on center stage. He pulled his hat bib down low and ran to his personalized yellow Chevy that stood out like in this neighborhood like some buck teeth. Hiding his face did nothing but prove his shame because everybody knew he was in there all night long. Wasn't no hiding! Everybody and their momma knew that that sour lemon Chevy sitting on 30's was LA's. The whole block had not only seen but reported it.

Three neighborhood black girls who had rounded up everybody that morning, telling all who would listen about LA's secret endeavors, still sat on the porch waiting across the street on the sideline waiting on his red ass to come out.

What was the problem with so many black men going to the other side? A black woman needed a black man.

They had sat around, talking, and wanting to know. They all stopped conversating when he emerged. Each one made sure that he saw them watching him. He put his face down, disgraced, and should have been as he jumped in his car and sped off.

Grabbing up his black C.D. case, in plain view, sat the brown paper bag with the key of dope that he had accused Kat of stealing and beat her over.

LA just stared, still lost.

More confused than ever!

***

Somedays Bree thought back to life before Quent. She could not imagine ever going back to that. She knew she could not live without him. She did not know what was going on with her, or who she was becoming, then it hit her.

The reality caused Bree to finally see the truth and know that a change had to be made before Quent thought the same thing and took his own actions. So out of desperation, she started to calm down. More than life itself, she did not want to lose Quent, and without trying, that was what she was doing.

She did not see anything wrong with the shit she was doing at first, but when she did take a look in the mirror. Bree was thanking God for herself self-awareness and that she had not gone too far.

The love Bree had for Quent was almost unreal. Never would she have thought that it was possible for another person to become her world. She ate, slept, and shit all for Quent. He was her life.

"Baby! It's Friday. What do you want to do tonight?" Bree shocked; Quent, asking him that when he had got up that morning. The normal routine was Bree lying, saying she did not have the energy when it came to them going out. She would claim she did not want to leave the house, and then as soon as he was out the door, she would sneak out right behind him, following him.

At first, he was mad but got over it quickly as he remembered and felt all the trauma she had experienced. He was doing nothing, so to show her that when she followed him, he always made sure that she stayed with him.

And never lost her, even though he always spotted her and could have easily left her behind. He was trying to prove that he was all hers and that he was not doing anything wrong.

That he loved her and only her.

Quent had felt bad after his episode with Ashanti, so bad that he felt guilty when he was going to confront her with the news he had found out from the doctor about her secret hysterectomy. That guilt kept their secrets safe until she was ready to share it. He felt in due time, all would come to light.

While having dinner at Justin's that night, Quent's phone would not stop ringing each time he picked it up and pressed end, silencing the call. That was not the first time Bree had noticed him doing that to that forever ringing phone.

Quent had always been a busy man. But damn! Paranoia was sneaking back up, threaten to bite her on the ass.

145

'Who was that calling his phone?'
'Was it a girl who keeps calling?"
'Was he cheating on her?'

So many questions were running through her head, questions that she did not have a positive answer to. She did not want to believe it, but the signs were showing.

'And one had to read and pay attention to the signs', she thought.

Quent noticed the dark cloud that stormed over Bree's eyes every time she looked at the phone as it rung. He hoped to God that she did not think the reason he was not answering it was because it was somebody calling that should not have been.

Because that was not the case, by far. It was nobody but Ross. He just did not want to answer it, disturbing what they had going on.

He just wanted to spend this time and this night with his wife, without interruptions. He, on purpose, went to the restroom, leaving his phone on the table, knowing that Bree would go through the call log. But he wanted her to, so she could have reassurance.

He stayed long enough for her to go through the entire phone.

When he got back, the phone was face down, instead of face up how he had left it.

"Your phone rung," she was all smiles. Back bright and happy, go lucky.

"Who was it, babe? Ross ass again?"

"I don't know. I didn't answer it."

"Why not?"

"Baby, I trust you."

'Do you?' Quent silently asked. That should not have been an issue, but it was a big one.

"It was probably somebody from the club wondering where you are on a Friday night. You know how they cannot handle anything without my man present."

"Well, whoever will just have to wait. I'm with my baby."

The mere mention of the word baby caused Bree's grin to instantly faded.

The next morning Bree woke up earlier to find Quent gone.

Where the hell had he jumped up to?

She was now almost positive that he was really cheating on her, until that afternoon when Quent strutted in the house with his swag fully loaded, clad in a wifebeater with a big tattoo on his shoulder.

The picture was clear.

It was her, except she looked light on his light skin. Under the picture read, 'Bree wife for life,' Bree broke down crying.

All doubts were erased like paintings over bad writings on the wall. She was sure her man was not cheating on her and would never cheat on her nor ever leave her. Anxiety seemed to lift and float away. The marriage would work. She could stop worrying. Now, all they need was a baby. Maybe she should consider Shuga's plan. Thinking it over in her head, it did not sound so bad.

***

He did it again.

Almost two weeks had passed, and Shuga had not heard from Cage since their night together. Repeating her same actions, she called and called him without stopping. Every time her phone rung, she jumped and about had a heart attack, hoping it was Cage. Only it never was. Once again, she had played herself, like the hoes she talked about.

When was she ever going to learn?

Pitifully, Shuga looked in the mirror at her nappy head.

Since that night, she and TL had their run in when he dashed beer on her, she had not gotten her hair fixed.

That was how down she was, cause Shuga kept her hair freshly premed and wrapped.

Hearing her phone ring, she jumped up and ran to the wall, grabbing it up, looking at the caller I.D., disappointed that it was only Kresa.

"Yeah!" She answered, super dry.

"Bitch!" Kresa screamed, excited, and hyper, and Shuga could tell, without seeing her, could tell that she was bouncing all around. "Why you let them niggas film you doing that shit?"

"What the fuck is you talking about?"

"Bitch, they dubbed that tape and got bout a million copies floating and that shit all around Mechanicsville, Bowen Homes, Simpson Road, all the way out in the Dec. Bitch that shit just everywhere! At first, when Ne-Ne and them told me, I was like n'all I didn't think it was yo ass, cause yo hair wasn't in that

147

wrap but all wild and shit, but then I saw them bears on yo thighs. Bitch I'm the one that picked them out, so I knew that was yo' ass."

"Bitch, what tape? Kresa, what the fuck is you talking about?"

"Bitch, I'm talking about how them niggas videotaped yo' ass with Cage and some other nigga fucking in yo' bedroom. Hoe, why would you let them do that shit? I hope you got some major ends for that one. Couldn't been me still."

"Bitch, ain't no fucking niggas videotaped me doing shit."

"Yes, they did! Yes, they did! I know how your bedroom look! It showed Cage fucking you all in the ass, and your hair was wet. See, I knew you was gone say that! I got something for that. That's why I took my last twenty and bought a copy. Them niggas making hella cheese selling off yo ass with that tape. If I would've had a ride, I would've popped up at yo crib. But you need to come sees this."

"Hold on bitch, my line beeping," Shuga said, saved by the bell, wondering why Kresa was calling her making up shit or repeating inaccurate information that Ne-Ne's hating ass had started. They probably were all jealous caused they had heard. Cage was fucking with her. That is what that shit had to be, Shuga concluded then clicked her phone. "Hello?"

"Somebody called from this number?" The caller asked.

Excited, she almost blurted Cage's name but did not want to appear as she really was.... desperate.

"Who is dis?"

"Eric."

"Eric?" *Who the fuck is Eric?* Shuga thought.

"Yeah."

Then she remembered, "How long has that been. Boy, you done made me wait forever and a day."

"Shawty, I just got back in town yesterday, and ain't too many people got this number."

"Hold on," Shuga clicked her line. "Kresa?"

"Yeah bitch you on the way?"

"Sure," she lied. "I'll be through later on. I got a call." Shuga hung on Kresa.

"What's up?" She seductively asked.

"What's up, shawty? But can I get a name?"

"Eric, this is Shuga. What have you been up to?"

"Shuga? Kresa's friend? Oh, hell, n'all. I gotta go."

"Say, I didn't call you for her."

"Then why you calling?"

"To see what was up with you. I heard you making major moves, and a bitch wanted to see what was good."

"Ha-Ha!" He laughed. "You fooled up! Yall must be with that ole three-way shit. Is that why you clicked over."

"Ain't nobody with them childish ass games. I thought you was ready for a real one."

"Shawty, ain't you, Kresa friend, though?"

She did not answer, "Are you with her or something?"

He did not answer. "Is this yo' number?"

"Duh? I answered, didn't I?"

"Shawty, I 'ma hit you back a little later."

***

Ray J was debating back and forth in his head for hours but still did not know what to do. He had never been good at making big decisions solely on his own, and whenever he did, he chose the wrong one, and that was a big part of the reason why his life was so fucked up today. He never knew what to do. If Pam's sorry ass would not have helped him smoke up all his money and then put him back out, leaving him high and dry and not the kind of high he liked. He would not be in this shit. Now he was stuck, not knowing what to do.

Should he?

Should he not?

He was confused.

One part was telling him no, while the other part was screaming go-go-go!

Go on and take that 100 dollars that detective Marshall was offering him and be free since Redman had got murked he had not had no one to look out for him. Redman was good people. Was the only dope boy that kept him hooked up on a guaranteed type level? He did not have to put up with Pam and her bullshit when Redman was alive, cause that nigga always had his back. His thoughts exaggerated.

Redman getting murked was the reason he was sitting right here in jail now. He told himself. Times had gotten so hard for Ray J that after Pam had put him out, he had resorted back his old hustle. Stealing from the Dollar

General store and selling the stuff he stole to the neighborhood women on their first of the month check day. That hustle was slow now because he had gotten used to smoking more dope and needed more money to buy that dope. So trying to speed up, he had started going to the same store more and more, so often that not only did he know all the employees, but worst they knew his stoned out looking ass and what tricks he was up to.

To nip this petty shit in the bud, a set up was made. One day as soon as the Dollar General store cashier saw him strut his poor ass in, she done as planned and alerted the store manager, who came to the front and called the police and waited on him to make his move. Loaded down, Ray J got ready to roll; right before he reached the exit door, security was ready to lunge at him. They were attempting to snatch him up, but he did not see it their way. He would not go out like no pussy. There was no way he was not going out without a fight. Amped up, he used everything his little ninety-pound weak ass body to try to fight his way free through two big ass dudes that were waiting to take him in. For a minute, it looked like he was about to get away; after all, he was a nigga fighting for his freedom. He developed a strength even he did not know he pressure, but his strength would not prevail. The only thing that he ended up winning were two big boy charges, assault on officers, to go along with the petty shoplifting charge.

With or without a bond, he knew his broke ass was stuck. So mentally, he was prepared to lay down until the judge freed him on his own recognizance. But then the unexpected hit him; when he got booked, they did an NCIC check, and his prints came back as a wanted fugitive. He did not know what to do.

Ray J had long ago violated his probation on like he first month they gave it to him, from a dirty urine, but that was petty. Everything he done was petty. So, he already knew of the V.O.P. warrant that was it. But that was not what they were talking about. They were locking for him because he was a wanted man in connection with the murder of one Torenzo B. Gaye, better known in the hood as Redman.

'Damn, them people though 'HE' had killed Redman.'

Ray J could not see it! There was no fucking way he was going down on no type of murder charge, connection, or what the hell ever they were saying. Even as fucked up as he was, he was not that dumb to let them believe they could stick that shit on him. They said the motive was a robbery. He tried to make them see logic that if he had robbed this known big-time drug dealer, why would he be out stealing from the Dollar General?

He was out stealing because his ass was broke, that was why.

They kept feeding him Little Debbie snack cakes and Cokes and giving him cigarette after cigarette while playing good cop, bad cop.

Finally, the breakdown came: Options:

1) Go ahead, tell on whoever really done the shit. Get all the bribes he knew they were offering, maybe work out a little more, plus have all his charges dropped.

2)Gone stay. Be quiet. Do not talk. They had nothing big on him. Do his little ninety days in the work release for his probation violation. Get out and find LA. Get some real money from him and make him look out for him with a few threats. Make him see that he owed him his life.

But nope, that would not work, because LA did not take threats. He would just take Ray J out for even coming at him like that.

Ray J was stuck. He would have to do what was best for him in the end. So, he decided to go with option 1. Telling himself that he was not snitching, just looking out for his boy Redman. The only somebody whoever looked out for him, so in return, he was doing Redman one last favor, showing thanks. He told himself his loyalty lay with Redman, not LA anyway.

He pepped talked himself. Then the crisp one-hundred-dollar bill was in his pocket.

Chapter 19

Shuga did not have the jump on how *'it'* happened. *'It'* was too much for her to fully comprehend.... and for a brief moment, she had actually felt bad. She felt terrible only until she remembered how Kresa had laughed in her face to diss her and made her feel bad talking about that so-called porn of hers. Sniggling and giggling on how hilariously trashy *'Queen Shuga'* had been caught.

All Shuga could now think was, laugh now- cry later, bitch.

So, with that thought, she would show her just how trashy she could be and continued sucking Eric's big, black ten-inch dick. It was so huge with a crook that had her going crazy. She watched in amazement as it grew even bigger. This fuck was going to be a good one for more than one reason. Not only was she getting back at Kresa with the man she was so in love with, but also ole boy seemed to her that he could handle his business. She would soon find out.

All the shit she had told Kresa about this same nigga just a few months ago was long forgotten. In fact, she was thinking like Kresa now. That she could take him away from the bullshit and his baby momma. That all he needed was the right woman.

For the next three weeks straight, Eric had become a permanent fixture at Shuga's. Even though he was not the big man around the 'A' or flossing, well-known like she liked them. He was moving a little something-something. Really, none of that mattered, because Shuga, for once in her life, found herself happy. Some days, she did wonder how she had found love with Eric, her best friend's wannabe man. She could not figure it out. Her only logical thought was that the devil was trying to steal her joy with these negative thoughts, so she was not going to wreck her brain, thinking that way anymore.

All she knew is that she had him, and he meant a lot to her and was worth ending Kresa's childhood long friendship.

Eric was *'that'* nigga in Shuga's eyes. She knew with a bitch like her at his side, it would not gone be long before they saw better days. Eric had big plans that Shuga was going to stand by his side and support.

The first of the month came around, and Shuga went to collect Mineta's child support money, having problems from Mark's wannabe ass, as usual. Coming with those same tired wore-out scripted lines that he was going through a tough period... having a hard time... looking at her with puppy dog sad eyes as if she would offer him some change. He was always having a hard time, a hard time that would never end. In actuality, the nigga just had too many kids with not enough income, so his ass could not take care of them. When is the class going to be in session so that no good niggas can learn to do the math and figure out that it really is cheaper to buy a condom than to be made to take care of a kid for eighteen years -sometimes plus if they were lazy. And nine times out of ten, if their daddy is lazy, they might inherit that bone. She had also confronted him just remembering about that self-made fake hundred-dollar bill that he had paid her with last time. But of course, he denied his shady ways with all sincerity, putting it on everything he love that he would never do no shit like that. Even though she could see in his shifty eyes that he was lying. She just did not have time to continue this charade with him, as long as he came with the correct money. She would check every single dollar in his face from now on. If shit did not look up to par, she would threaten him with the name of the child support place to get him walking straight... At least for a little while.

She loaned Eric the money she had picked up, two-thousand dollars, for his come up, and he promised to bring her back double.

Truly, she did not care about getting no double back return cause money came easy for her. She saw something in Eric that she had never seen in any other nigga that she had dealt with. She would let him know that when he returned. She was so into him that his money did not matter. What was hers was his and vice versa.

But then, the unexpected happened. Two whole days had went by, and Eric had not called her, not even once. She had put him on speed dial and had attempted to reach him over a hundred times with nothing but rings. The nigga was not getting back at her. All kinds of thoughts raced through Shuga's head. What he would never know was concern was her biggest.

'*Was he alright?*' She needed to know.

He may have been hurt- that had to be it because Eric was hers, and they were in love and building something. There was no way he would not answer the phone for her, right? She would not believe anything other than that and had even started calling around checking hospitals for his whereabouts.

When the results on that yield zero on that, she started back dialing his number, leaving message after message, begging for nobody ass Eric to call her. After the begging subsided, she became angry, finally realizing that bum ass Eric had played her for a measly two grand. Shuga felt so low and was now desperate. She concocted a master plan; she would blackmail him. She started leaving message after message, this time saying that she was going to tell Erica everything if he did not get back to her. She was obsessed. She did not stop until it was announced in her ear that the mailbox was full, therefore not allowing any more of those useless threats.

What Shuga was unaware of and would never understand was that Eric and Erica had a gangsta relationship.

Eric stayed fucking on her, but in the end, he always returned home with Erica waiting to always let him in. Erica knew full well what was up. He did not keep secrets from her about all the hoes he fucked. The crazy thing was Erica understood his actions, and by her being led by a low self-esteem, she believed that all men cheated and that it was okay. After all, these were his same actions for the last fifteen years now. He was not going to change, and she felt she did not have a choice. Her alternatives were limited. He gave her ass 'my way' or the highway type of deal. Unattractive, at twenty-eight with seven kids, what was she to do?

So, she took it and felt they were down with each other like that, through thick and thin. This was her way of showing him that she had his back. Eric's phone was not the only thing blowing up. Shit was about to get serious. More days of that went by, and finally, Eric's phone answered. Well, not him, but his better half.

"Bitch! Will you fucking' stop! Got damn! Hoe don't you have anything to do, besides call this phone? Bitch get a life! Don't you realize Eric knows you are callin', Boo. He does! So, Bitch realize it's over!"

"Who dis?" Shuga could not believe the shit that was being said.

"Erica! Like yo, ass ain't know what it is and what it will always be! He is here! We are back together once again. Boo! So, get that message. Stop wasting yo' time leaving messages on his phone! Don't call no mo' bitch!"

"Fuck you, hoe! You Scobby-Doo need a snack looking bitch!" Hurt, Shuga could only think to resort to name-calling.

Erica only laughed, feeling she had the upper hand. "You played yo 'self hot girl! Thanks for them, two Gs. Eric got me a nice Gucci bag and our kids some stuff. Gotta go."

A Gucci bag? "Bitch please-" Shuga screamed, but the phone was already dead. *A Gucci bag?* I bet that bitch do not even know shit about no real Gucci.

Shuga called her back. She would not stop calling now... she could not stop. She was out of control. It was like she was gone in this obsession. Every chance she got, she just kept on calling and calling.... and calling, not even for Eric, now she called just to curse Erica out. Then Erica would curse her out. They would go back and forth, threatening each other to do this or that when they saw one another. Shuga did not care what she said over the phone lines cause Erica did not know who she as in real life or how she looked. She herself had only seen Erica a few times, and that was always in a crowd. All she knew was the fat neck bitch resembled a beast.

For days in and days out, Shuga sat home alone and sad moping around. She did not know why Eric had just bounced on her like that when she had not done anything but treat him good. The only excitement her life now consisted of was when she picked up her phone and dialed Eric's number to curse out the broke bitch he had chosen over her. She had just finished talking about how ugly their kids were -kids she had never laid eyes upon but did not care what she said when her doorbell rung interrupting her. She yanked the door open with an attitude, never thinking that one day it could be possible that she would have to make good on all those threats she had made recklessly.

"What do you want?" She screamed, asking a young girl who could not have been any more than thirteen or fourteen, and she had never noticed in the neighborhood.

The girl was just standing and did not respond back to her with words. Without warning, the girl grabbed a big chunk of Shuga's hair and snatched her out the doorway by it.

"What the fuck!" Shuga did not know what was going on or what was happening.

Fighter she was not, so she did not know what to do.

"What's all that shit you been talking about my muthafuckin kids hoe?" Shuga was quickly surrounded by a circle of unknown hoodrats, but that particular voice stood out.

She recognized it and almost shit her pants.

That voice belonged to Erica!

In no time flat, Shuga was mopped up on the concrete in the parking lot bruised and bloody. Erica had sat on top of her wearing her ass out. Shuga was pinned down and could not do anything even if she knew what to do. She was on the ground flat back, just kicking her legs up and down, screaming.

"Shuga! I'm on the phone with the police right now," Mineta yelled out the door, saving Shuga from more licks.

Universally, whenever a nigga hears the police coming, it seems to click in their minds to run. And that was just what the group did.

Shuga was left curled up laying on the ground in a fetal position, unable to move, even long after they had loaded up in the hoopty that brought them and bounced.

Kim came over, the only neighbor who was looking and decided to help her up. Shuga had been living in The Overlook long enough that she knew everyone, and everyone knew her, and what they knew of her they did not like. So, they laughed at her getting her ass kicked and thought it was about time.

Shuga limped in the house beat up with a busted lip and knots everywhere, just swollen the fuck, up. "Shuga! Auntie Kresa had called, and I told her you was outside fighting. She on her way over. She said she just gone hop a cab."

Kresa made it running around the corner from the cab she had ditched without paying, just as the police did.

"Bitch, what the fuck happened over here, hoe?"

"Her and Erica them done got the fighting!" Kim busted out.

"Erica?" Kresa looked funny.

"Eric's baby momma," Kim further supplied, and Shuga had to get Kim out of her house cause she would spill the beans and tell it all. Kim didn't know and would have never guessed with all the tries in the world that Eric was

Kresa's man first, and that Shuga went behind her so-called best friend's back and started fucking him. That was a secret she did not want to let out the bag.

"I'll call you, Kim," Shuga said, rushing her off. She had not planned on telling Kresa that it was Erica who jumped her. *'Damn'!*

As the police walked in, Shuga began making up her story. "I was walking from my car when a girl name Erica was over one of my neighbor's apartment." She lied.

"Do you know which one?" The police interrupted.

"No. They asked me did I fuck with a girl name Kresa."

"Me?" Kresa asked, shocked, but on the inside was happy that some shit was being started behind her nasty ass.

"Yeah, you. I told them that I was your *'best'* friend, and they jumped on me, girl," she lied, looking sincerely into Kresa's eyes. "They said they looking for you, and gone get you next. Worst they said."

"I didn't even know that Erica knew about me," Kresa said while feeling that for Eric's woman to be fighting because of her, and she had not seen Eric in months, she had to have a mental hold on him. "I'm so sorry! I forgot how much of a bitch made nigga Eric is. He probably just mad that I won't fuck with him no more! We gone get his ass. Believe that, baby! And her too!" Kresa just knew since Erica was fighting about her that Eric must have told Erica how he truly felt, and she was in her feelings. That thought alone gave her hope that she could get him back. And this time he would be all hers. She just wondered why he had not called. He had changed his number, but she had not changed hers.

"Ma'am. Do you have a full name and description of your assailant?"

"Erica Daniels," Kresa supplied, then Shuga went into detail, drawing a full picture of how ugly Erica was as the description.

"Would you like to follow me to the station to take out an arrest warrant for assault?"

"Would I? Hell yeah!" Shuga had not even though that far. *'Let that animal rot in a jail cage where she belonged,'* she silently laughed.

Kresa rode with Shuga to the police station, where she was asked to identify Erica from an old mug shot. She called Kresa over to share a laugh. "Look at this booger bear looking muthfucka. This bitch got a beard! Bitch what the fuck is in that nigga Eric's head? He can do so much better." Shuga looked longingly.

Kresa walked over laughing, feeling like maybe, Shuga could possibly accept Eric and not bad mouth him no more. Even though Kresa told anyone who would listen, she was not fucking with him no more. That was so far from what her heartfelt.

If she only knew.

Kresa looked at the picture, still laughing but abruptly stopped as she scanned the contact sheet spotting a phone number. Something she had not had since Eric changed his after that night at the club.

"Aye, I got that bitches social security number and her birthday," Kresa bragged once they were back in the car. She withheld the fact she had also retrieved a phone number. Something was telling her not to share her plan to get back with Eric just yet. "I'm gone do the do to this bitch she don't know who she fucking with. Bitch gone have warrants coming from everywhere."

Shuga just laughed, happy Erica was soon gone be away from Eric.

Kresa could not wait to get home. She was ready to start part one of her get back with Eric plan. She ran to her bed and spread out, dialing the phone number from the jail's contact sheet.

Like Shuga, she too was sprung. Eric, who had been waiting on Erica to get back home to collect the three youngest kids she'd left him earlier, picked up on the first ring.

"Nigga why in the fuck did you have your monkey jump on my girl?" Kresa asked, full of confidence that it was all about her while thinking he would be happy to hear her voice.

Eric was about to drop a bomb on that ass.

***

Within two hours of Ray J turning snitch, over twenty police cars surrounded LA's house. He had just made it home to find Kat packing her stuff.

He wanted to tell her he was sorry, maybe get on his knees and beg for her to forgive him, but his pride would not let him.

Standing there, seeing Kat look like the elephant man, made his heartache. "Listen, you ain't got to go nowhere. If you need to be by yourself, then I'll leave till we sort things out. If we sort things out. But you ain't got to go nowhere. I 'ma leave."

She did not answer him. She went on packing, pretending he was not there. He had hurt her to her core when he had accused her of stealing. And not just stealing but stealing dope. Something she wanted nothing to do with ever in life. She had already decided if she really wanted her life to change, then she would have to be the one to make the first steps towards the direction of change.

Even though she did not have a place to go or even a thought to where she could possibly go, all she knew was she was not staying at his house with him in it or not.

She could always tuck her tail and go back to Shuga's. She would accept her back for a couple reasons. One Shuga would be able to gloat with some '*I told you so's,*' and two Kat could go right back to being Mineta's live-in babysitter. But she was not trying to go back. She was only pushing forward, and to be around someone that would throw up every little mistake would only make her regress. She still carried the name and number of the shelter that her counsel from the prison had recommended she check out. She guessed that would be her next destination.

"Do you hear me?" LA had still been talking. He screamed at her right as one of Georgia's infamous, no-knock warrants were executed, and the front door was flattened out.

Home invasion was LA's first thought. The jack boys would sure to want to hit a lick from him. He ran to the edge of the steps. It was not what he thought. Anywhere, everywhere all he saw were men in black.

Policemen in black.

A raid? He assumed.

He did not have a chance to hide or toss the gun that he carried in the small of his back.

"Put your hands up!"

"Don't move!"

"Put your hands on top of your head!"

All kinds of directives were being yelled at him. Then, he got rushed and bought down to the ground hard. They took the gun, handcuffed him, and carried him to the car bucking. He was cursing Kat, calling her every crack head bitch, cheap hoe, and nasty slut name he could think of. He knew she had pulled a dirty trick by calling the law on him for beating her ass.

If he only knew.

He would not stop ranting and raving about Kat until he saw them carting her out in cuffs too.

Now he sat bewildered.

Kat was being taken in for violating her parole. In the state of Georgia, two felons cannot reside together.

When LA got to the station, he did not have anyone to call. Turk, his boy, was dead. Kat was here locked up too. Not many choices for a nigga that rode solo and felt he did not need nobody in his life. A nigga who thought he was above the world now needed someone. At least one person that had his back

Then he thought in desperate mind mode. He could call Rio.... as usual, desperation had him do it.

"Listen, I got picked up! I need you to find out how much my bond is and make it happen ASAP!"

"Sure thing Papi-" Rio was still talking, but LA had already hung up. He did not want to hear none of that bullshit. He said what needed to be done, what was left to talk about.

At that time, he did not know he would be charged with a murder because he was still waiting to be booked. Out of his peripheral view, he saw a fast walking gait that he knew. Dude was getting it too.

It was dope head Ray J from round da way, looking all nervous.

"Ray J? What's up nigga?"

Ray J's eyes popped as he looked over at LA, seated on a booking bench. LA, so self-absorbed, had not caught the look of fear Ray J was permeating.

"Oh-oh. What's up?" He stuttered. "I-I'm bonding out!"

"Aight. Holla. Nigga!" Ray had started jogging out and almost tripped on a step running up, moving so fast.

LA did not pay it no mind, because that's what a nigga did leaving jail. Run. Shit, He was gone get somewhere too, just as soon as Rio came through for him.

LA got processed only to get his feelings hurt. He was officially charged with the first-degree murder of Torenzo B. Gaye and was being held without a bond. That was when shit came into focus. He remembered the look that had registered from Ray J's face.

Dude had traded him out.

Ray J had snitched him out to get a *get out of jail free* card. He should have been realized there was no one there to make a bail bond for Ray J's cracked out ass. He did not have one single person to make sure he had a toothbrush, much less a cosigner to make sure his raggedy-ass made it back to court.

'Never leave any witnesses that can cause yo ass to be judged by twelve- leave behind the kind that has to be carried by six,' popped in LA's head, hearing his brother's voice.

Nigga's is dirty. He should have smoked his ass. Now he was fucked up.

LA was lead to his cell, where he fell out dead to the world from frustration. Mad at Kat all over. Love had his ass blind. Love will do that shit. Have you all thrown off of your square. The point of focus just lost.

Next thang you know, LA was running in a living nightmare, where Rio was whispering something to him. It sounded so real that he sat up, but Rio could not be here with him in his jail cell. Yet he opened his eyes. He had to see how his mind was playing tricks on him. And when he did, Rio spoke. "Papi, you didn't have no bond. So, I came down here."

LA looked like a bin-ya-bend crazy house patient. He could not possibly be seeing what was right before his eyes. But he was.

No, he was delusional.

"Yeah, baby, it's me. I came down here for you, boo," Rio continued. "I got arrested for jaywalking and told them that I couldn't make my bond, so I could come back here with you. Just for you! I know you going through it. Don't worry, though, I'm here for you. We gone get through this together. I won't leave yo' side."

Looking at Rio's big black bald-headed ass, without all that exotic shit. No weave hair. Just a nigga staring back at him. It took him back to his youth and made him think about his momma's boyfriend- the one that use to molest him. He did not want to see Rio looking like Mario, his real self.

Reality of what he was but wanted no one to know shot in his veins and through his entire being. He could not handle exposing his secret- that he sought the comfort of a man's arms.

Confused- humiliated-embarrassed, all caused him to swiftly jump up and attack Mario, beating him down. It took a little more to get Mario than it had Kat; after all, Rio was still a man.

Eventually, the guards were called, and they came and drug LA off Rio.

But not before a crowd had gathered.

A few folks had seen Rio waltz his ass up in LA's cell when he first got to the back. Some believed that Rio was LA's shit call; others said that Rio was a stalker of dope boys and did not believe that LA would go out homo thug. The same ones that protected LA's reputation were the same ones that had something to hide themselves.

"That's right, beat that punk straight!"

"Y'all bet not let his faggot ass back out in population!"

"We gone get his ass too!"

The crowd threatened.

"You better stay on protective custody bitch!"

"And read ya' Bible till ya' straight!"

Mario was not only physically hurt but emotionally as well. He then decided he would make his bond.

Chapter 20

The day after Kresa learned the truth of her best friend's infidelity, she had come up with a plan. Keeping the future in focus, she called Shuga, and it took everything in her to act like nothing had happened. Playing Shuga, Kresa asked her if she would take her to pay her Metro PCS cell phone bill, and the whole time she had to keep reminding herself of the bigger picture.

Shuga, out of her guilty feelings, did.

Normally, she would be complaining about how high gas prices are.

They were in the car, and Kresa keep cool, even though she did not want to, but she stuck to her bigger plan. Rather than fussing and fighting or pulling out hair. Even though she wanted too! She had actually drawn blood from biting her tongue, trying hard to hold it.

"Damn! Yo' face still fucked up!" Kresa exaggerated. She might not could say what she wanted, but she was going to say something.

"Forreal?" Shuga asked, jumping to look in the mirror.

"Don't worry. She on the hit list," Kresa lied. The only one that was on her list was Shuga's ass, and she would not be made aware of that just yet.

"Whatever happened with that nigga you met at the club?" Kresa asked after a while.

"Big Cee? Bitch! I told you I stopped fucking with him."

"Yeah, but you never said why."

"Bitch, he started stalking me after one night and wouldn't leave me alone. Bitch, I let him taste the honey and bay-bay!" She laughed. "But you know I wouldn't be fucking with him now anyway. Not after his boy did that foul ass shit to you."

"I feel ya. Loyalty everything."

"You ain't never lied," Shuga agreed, wondering once again why she ever fucked with Eric in the first place. She wanted to come out and tell Kresa, to let her know how wrong she was and how very sorry she felt, now. To let Kresa make that choice on if she wanted to continue their friendship.

But pride, along with fear of rejection, would not let her, so she continued with her scandalous secret, hoping that the shit would never surface.

But if she would have paid more attention to her foster mom all them days, she was preaching and trying to instill some sense into her, she would know that all things done in the dark will come to the light.

"Shit. Bitch, I gotta get some gas." Shuga said as she pulled up to a QuikTrip.

"Here," Kresa handed her a ten, just as Shuga had reached over for her purse from the backseat's floor. Kresa knew Shuga's greedy ass, like the back of her hand. She dropped the purse to take the money from her. Some things just never change and Shuga never turning down money was one of them.

"Thank you. Bitch, I'm kinda low. It's a whole nother month, before the first," she laughed.

'I'm sure you are dumb bitch! You gave that sorry ass nigga yo, fucking child support money,' Kresa silently ranted.

As soon as Shuga was in the store, Kresa reached around the backseat to Shuga's purse. Kresa dug around in it until she found the blackberry. She copied three very important numbers out of its directory, then threw the phone back in the cluttered purse. Remembering something else, she felt around in the purse once again, finding about two hundred dollars in twenties. Kresa stuffed them in her bra.

'Fuck that bitch!' Kresa smirked to herself. *'Let this hoe learn a lesson. Never make enemies with a bitch that know all ya business.'*

Before Shuga could make it back home, Bree had called letting her know that they were back home at her house from taking Mineta shopping, spoiling her even more. So Shuga beelined to Bree's Brookhaven community. Shuga got out and looked around at all the huge houses, now this was an address she would love to have on her driver's license. She sauntered in the newly interior designed home, and her and Bree got lost in conversation. Bree went on and on a million a miles per minute, loving to get the chance to talk. It wasn't like she had friends until Mineta walked up with a picture of Quent and his fraternity brothers.

"Look, Shuga."

"What I tell yo fast ass about interrupting grown folks?" Shuga snapped, and Mineta rolled her eyes and walked off pouting.

"You ain't got to get smart with me. I was just gone show you a picture of Chris."

"Chris? Give me that," and Shuga snatched the photo out of Mineta's hands.

"Girl, that's Quent and his frat brothers."

"Quent went to college?"

"Yes! You make it sound like my man dumb. He has a B.A. in business from Morehouse for your information. Why do you think his club does so well?"

Then, Shuga saw just what Mineta had. Chris smiling, a little younger, a little slimmer, but it was definitely Chris. "Do you know any of them?" Shuga asked, caring only to know if she knew one forreal.

"Yes, I know all of them, and no, I am not hooking you up with any of them!" Bree laughed.

"Bitch, I don't need to be hooked up. I already had him. I just wanted to know if you knew his crazy ass?"

"And all I was saying, slut, was I know that they are not your type. Which one you talking about?"

"Him. Chris!" Shuga pointed.

"Chris? You went out with Chris! When!"

"You act like you don't believe me."

"It just seems like if you would have dated Chris that 'you' would have kept Chris."

"Chris is lame as fuck, then he started stalking me!"

"Chris is sweet! He just not all ghetto-like you like them."

"Whatever! Yes, I had gave his as a taste and bout had to get a restraining order just for him to leave me alone." Shuga bragged.

"Oh, it seems like 'you' would have tried to keep him!"

"Why you keep saying that? I told you that muthaucka crazy!"

"Cause he paid, crazy or not, and that's what you go after, the bank!"

"Bitch, I summed him up, and his total came to fronting! He was just another fronting as nigga in this world of plenty. Talkin bout he was Da Snowman's bodyguard or some shit!"

Bree burst out laughing, "A bodyguard? For Da Snowman? He told you that? N'all!"

"I knew he was frontin'!"

"I think they like cousins or something," Bree was still laughing. "I can't believe he told you that."

"Yes, bitch! He did that!"

"A bodyguard? He must have wanted to downgrade himself."

"Downgrade? What you mean?"

"I mean, how much can being Da Snowman's bodyguard really pay a millionaire?"

"I don't know" Shuga looked confused. The conversation had her lost, and she was getting anxious. "What are you talking about? Did you just say, millionaire? Who?"

"Listen to the little whore. I am not about to be telling all that man's business. He is Quent's friend. But you fucked up, I will let you know that! He is a trader!"

"A trader? What the fuck is a trader?"

"I don't know exactly what it is he does, but it has to do with investments. He barely works and makes millions."

"*Millions?*"

"Yes, *millions!*"

"You're lying!"

"No, I am not! *Why would I?*"

Shuga looked sick as Bree went on talking and telling all the business that she has just said she was not about to tell, including how he just met some chick and bought her a Corvette for her birthday.

Shuga was so sick, she wanted to throw up. She had fucked up big.

Then to top it off, Bree added, "and if you still got his number, you need to lose it! Don't try to call that man now that you know he the black Bill Gates. Gone head and lose it because Chris seem to be in love with that girl and they about to get married. And you know how I feel about women trying to break up marriages."

"*Married?*" Shuga's stomach flipped. She did not want to hear no more of this depressing conversation.

Shuga had been in her house searching for Chris number, not caring what Bree had advised if she could get him back, she was. Only she could find his number nowhere.

Disappointed, she flopped down on her couch, right as a knock came to the door. She jumped excited, thinking that Bree had called Chris and told him they had been talking about him, and he showed up.

Walking to the door, thanking the gods for sending Chris, she opened her door not to see a black colored Range Rover, but a bent the fuck up Cadillac. With Mark's stupid as waving wildly for her.

Shuga could not phantom know what the hell Mark wanted. He had said he was coming up the last time she saw him. She told him to holla at her then. So maybe he had come up. He knew not to come otherwise.

Maybe she could get a handbag out of his as to make her feel better.

***

Like all those locked up, Kat and LA got into the jail game and found ways to communicate. LA had paid nine trustees to pass letters for them through the trays at mealtimes. Kat had to wait for the court to find out if her probation would be reinstated. She only had about six months left. She didn't think they'd make her do it, but she did not know what the State of Georgia had planned for her.

LA was still on lockdown, even though Mario had bonded out. The jail still kept him in the hole because of the severity of the crime in which he was charged and the vicious act of violence he had committed upon his first day.

Five days down, and he was called out back in to see the state's doctor. It was always routine that the jail's check you initially upon entrance of the facility.

"I just want to go over your test results," the doctor said without looking up.

"Yeah-yeah-yeah," LA said nonchalantly; he was rushing too. Wanting to get back to his cell to finish a book that one of the trustees had slide him under the door.

'Hard Knock Life,' by Tamika Bumpass and it was a book he could not put down.

The doctors ran down his medical history, all that he had heard a thousand times. He was a fan of fried, greasy high in sodium foods, so his blood pressure was high, and they were putting him on a pill he had never heard of to help control it. His iron was low, for that he would get a pill too.

He was about to stand up and leave when the doctor told him of his HIV status, which was positive, and that he would start him on Abacuvir tonight.

LA could not believe his ears. *HIV?*

"Whoa. Whoa. Whoa. I'm HIV positive?"

The doctors just looked at him like he should have already known. LA might as well been talking to himself cause the doctor did not respond. He was tired of dealing with criminals, anyway. He did not go to school all those years for this bullshit! Even though he barely made it, he had, and that is what he looked at, and that was what counted.

"That's it." The doctor called the guard to escort LA back to his lockdown cell, where his tray, with a letter from Kat, awaited with the book on his bunk.

LA did not finish the book. He no longer cared what was in it.

Kat had went to the doctor to, but her news was different. Totally different. Kat had found out she was pregnant…

But he did not read the letter. Did not care what it said.

His life was over!

Too much!

Could not handle it!

LA ripped his sheet off his mat, then tied the other one to sprinkle and the other to his neck.

Hours later, he was found dead hanging.

***

Marqueta was fye hot and took it almost personal that Quent had not left Bree for Ashanti. She even started co-conspiring with Ashanti against Bree. She hated Bree more than ever and did not want her brother with her another day.

"Let's call that siddity bitch up and till her yo ass pregnant." Marqueta squealed out with delight at her trifling idea.

"Bitch what!" Ashanti was down with it. She was still mad that Quent had once again played her.

"Yes, bitch! Let's make that pretty hoe jump out da fucking window or something. You know she ain't right in the head." Marqueta laughed while reaching for the phone.

"Hello," Bree answered.

Marqueta frowned, making a face of disgust, hating her white sound always got to be proper voice.

"Bree, this Marqueta."

"Hello, Marqueta."

Marqueta sucked her teeth; she could not stand this lady. "Bree listen," She faked concern. "I have someone who's over my house, looking for Quent."

"Looking for Quentin? Un-hun," Bree's heart raced. Automatically thinking it was some dudes, and it had something to do with drugs.

"So, I really need to talk to Quent. Is he there?" She asked, knowing he was not home and hoped that Bree was 'black' enough to inquire about what was going on. She acted so 'white' sometimes.

"No, but what do they want? Is it bad? I mean... what is it? Tell me!"

"Well, I don't know. Bree, I really don't know if I should tell you." Before Bree could speak, Marqueta added," But since you are his wife. You are going to have to know sooner or later, right?"

"Exactly. What is it?"

"Hold up. How about this? I'll just let her tell you."

"Her?" Bree was not liking this.

"Yeah. Especially, since you can't have any," Marqueta taunted, but Bree was so anxious she didn't catch it.

"Hello? Yeah. Dis Quent's wife?"

"Why, yes, it is?"

"Listen up, today I went to the doctor and found out I was pregnant." Bree could have died before the words were even said; she knew what was next. "By your husband, and I don't know if he told you that I thought I was, but it's been confirmed, and -"

Bree did not hear any more. Her brain could only compute one little word with so much meaning.

Pregnant?

Pregnant?

Pregnant? It just kept ringing in her head.

She was the one that needed to be pregnant by her husband. Then it clicked- what Marqueta had said.

'Especially since you can't have any.'

How did she know?

"God! Why! God! Why! Why! Why!" Bree screamed, so loud and evil that Ashanti nervously hung up the phone. No longer laughing. Wide-eyed, looking around like at any minute, something was going to happen.

Ashanti felt funny from the pits of her stomach. "Bitch, she is over there straight tripping! Going crazy! She is losing it. What is you gone do when Quent ask you about this shit?"

She had not thought of that. Then it hit her. "Oh, I 'ma say I didn't do it. I'm glad you ain't give her your name."

Then they both laughed, only Ashanti's was from bad nerves.

"Bitch, what was she saying?"

"I couldn't' understand the what. But the how! That bitch sounded like she was possessed. Like that girl from The Exorcist."

And that is what it was. Bree had sounded evil!

Marqueta laughed till her panties were wet, and she could not move any more, or she would pee all the way.

Ashanti giggled just to join in but was not feeling what they were laughing at.

"I know that bitch fye hot thinking Quent done got some bitch pregnant, and she can't have kids either."

"She can't have no kids?"

"No, I told you about that."

"No, you didn't!"

"Well yeah! They baby died during childbirth, and she had to have a hysterectomy."

"No, you ain't tell me that."

Marqueta laughed, "Yes, I did. You just don't remember."

Ashanti did not join this laugh. She no longer thought anything was funny.

***

Shuga flashed a fake smile hoping Mark came up, and if he had, maybe she would think about letting him be the man of her life. There was not anything else good coming her way. "What's up?"

"Where Mineta?" He looked around nervously and sweating, eyeing shit like he had just took a hit and beamed up to Scottie.

'Was he about to steal something?' She wondered as he scooped out her entertainment center. Shit was not looking right.

"Oh, so you remember her name today?" Shuga bent over laughing, flirtingly.

Swiftly, Mark grabbed her neck, yanking her up. "I don't see shit funny, hoe."

Shuga's laugher stopped. "Mark! What the fuck is wrong with you? My baby here! Nigga you better stop tripping! Just get out! Get the fuck out!"

Shuga tried to move, but he threw her to the steps. "Get up there. "He pointed to her bedroom "The secrets out!"

"Secret? What secret? What the fuck is you talking about nigga?

He pushed her down to her bed. "Who's Be-Be? Well, not who- everybody fucking knows who Be-Be is. No last name needed, but what is he to you?"

"Huh?" Shuga was thrown off.

"Or the doctor?"

"What?"

Shuga was stuck, feeling sick.

"Yeah, ya girl Kresa called us all, put us up on the game. Even gave me they numbers. I called they asses to-"

"What?" The shit had hit the fan. And it was stank.

All hell was about to break loose.

"The doctor stupid, but he did say that he was going to get a blood test for Mineta. Be-Be said he knew in his gut that Mineta wasn't his, and his girl Toni had been trying to get him to see that."

"That fucking white bitch! She lying!" That was all Shuga could say.

"N'all you lying! You lying bitch! You don't know who the fuck yo baby daddy is? Do you? Thought you had a good little hustle, Didn't you? And for a minute, you did You thought you had it all figured out. Didn't you? You don't know who yo baby daddy is! Do you?" He asked again, so mad that he was foaming out of the mouth.

Shuga did not answer none of the questions. "Get out! Get out! Get the fuck out!"

"N'all, I can't do that. Cause we gots a lil problem. Check dis, I been giving you a lot of my money. Hard-earned money. Money that I fucking needed! But not once did yo' trick ass see that I was trying to take care of a kid that ain't even mine. You's a dirty trifling bitch! All you did was try to squeeze money out of me, knowing I ain't have it!"

"What you want me to do?"

"Then, you give the money you claim Mineta needs so badly to a nigga that don't even want you. A nigga that used you! You a dumb bitch! A nigga in yo' face who want yo' sorry ass you wanna dog him." He grew angrier, howling. "Bitch take yo' clothes off!"

"No, the fuck I am not!"

Mark tackled her as she tried to run, then pinned her down. She started screaming, and Mineta ran into the room.

"Hey, baby, it's just daddy. Go watch T.V. and pull that door up." Mark spoke softly to Mineta.

"Okay, daddy," Mineta did as her *'daddy'* told her.

"You better be fucking quiet." He said, choking Shuga with one hand. Mark pulled his semi-hard dick out, never moving from the position he held her pinned down in. He pushed her little sleep booty shorts to the side and rammed his long skinny slimy feeling dick inside of Shuga's dry pussy. "You coulda been giving me this shit, acting all stuck up with this good pussy." Sweat was running everywhere from him.

Shuga whimpered, and tears ran down her face as he had his way with her. She did not want Mineta running in and seeing this, so she just kept quiet and gave in, silently crying at all that had been done and for what.

She felt his skinny dick swell and knew it would be over soon. She could hold out. Once he nutted inside of her, he stood up, and she was about to get off the bed, feeling disgusted and run to the shower when she was snatched back and pushed down.

"N'all bitch! You gon fuck me like you fucked them niggas on that tape. Yeah, Kresa, let me see that too! Take ya clothes off! All of um!"

Chapter 21

Bad news always spread quickly, and in a mere matter of minutes, everyone in the jail had heard that LA had killed himself.

No one knew exactly why. So, folks gave their own reasons, and stories floated.

He had not left a note. Just up and hung himself.

Jazzy, a hooker from Fulton Industrial, who knew Kat from back in the day, came over to console her. "Bitch, he was probably scared. I know plenty niggas who facing life that can't handle that. They'd rather take they self out!"

Kat did not respond. She just held her stomach, listening to Jazzy's non-comforting words.

"Who the fuck wanna live like an animal for the rest of they live? Shit, I'd kill myself too! That's why I live by the code- *'If you can't do the time, then don't do the crime, that'll get you that time!'*

Tears ran down Kat's face from Jazzy's insensitive words. Jazzy never really liked Kat, not understanding how anyone as pretty as she could be a straight-up dope fiend.

But secretly, jealously had her glad she was one.

Another secret, she was happy to hear the news of LA's demise. He was dead! Now Kat did not have nobody to take care of her. She would never luck up and get a nigga like LA ever again! Now the bitch would be back, just like them struggling. Vision blurry from her tears, Kat looked at Jazzy's sunken eyes and missing teeth and realized that was her future. That her next stop was back to life on the streets.

"Here bitch! This one on me. The next one you gone have to cop from Poochie." Jazzy handed Kat a nickel rock and an empty coke can that she would use to smoke the rock.

After she got fucked up. She was momentarily relieved. For those few moments, she was stress-free. Then minutes later, when her high came down, with it, so did reality.

Life was worse than before.

She was back hooked!

***

Bree kept hearing, *'pregnant-pregnant-pregnant,'* chanting over and over, while picturing Quentin in a delivery room with a faceless girl, then holding a baby and kissing the girl.

The girl wore her wedding ring.

She violently shook her head, to break those images. Only they would not fade.

Instead, more came.

They were now all laughing at her with Marqueta as the ringleader.

'Especially since you can't have any- Especially since you can't have any- Especially since you can't have any,' The girl kept saying it, then they all started screaming it at her.

She needed to focus---- on the road to as she ran a red light missing the back of a car bumper by inches.

She wanted to call Shuga.

Bree needed to call Shuga.

She should call Shuga, only she could not. She had rushed out the house so quick she had forgotten her phone.

Bree could not turn around.

She made it to her destination in what seemed like seconds. Without knowing how she had gotten there, she realized she was standing on the porch.

It was like she was floating.

Without knocking, she sauntered straight up in the house like it was hers.

"Who's pregnant?" She asked, a startled Marqueta.

No hesitations from Marqueta's end as she pointed straight to Ashanti.

The gun went from Marqueta's head to Ashanti's belly. Before Ashanti could say that they had just been playing on the phone, Bree loaded off in her stomach and left her slumped over.

Bree walked out the door like nothing had happened with Marqueta screaming to the top of her lungs.

***

A whole hour later, Shuga was still held hostage and tortured by Mark when Mineta knocked on the door.

"Shuga, I'm hungry!"

"Mark, move. I got to fix Mineta something to eat!"

"Wait a minute!"

"Shuga, I'm just gone fix me a sandwich," Mineta screamed through the door.

"Yeah, baby. Do that. Daddy'll be out in a minute." Mark moaned. "Fix you a sandwich."

"Mark, stop! Enough! I need to fix her some real food."

"Shut the fuck up and ride this dick! You like this shit. Don't you? Don't you?" He screamed, grabbing her hair, and punching her.

"Yeah, Mark. I like it."

"Ride it!"

Mark flipped her over, and Shuga began riding his dick. She bounced up on him for so long that she started coughing and could hardly breathe.

"Oh shit! Smoke!"

They looked around the room. It was filling with smoke. Shuga ran to the door and grabbed the knob.

Screaming, she yanked her hand back from the hot metal and grabbed a shirt off the floor to open the door.

"Mineta!" She screamed as a cloud of smoke knocked her in the face, coughing and eyes stinging, she could only see flames down the steps.

Mark pulled her back, rushing to get out of the house. As soon as Shuga made it to the bottom steps, she saw Mineta angel spread out on the floor. She looked unconscious.

"Where yo' fucking keys? I can't get this door opened." Mark screamed, turning at the knob, but unable to budge it, due to the deadbolt.

"On the table," Shuga yelled, picking up Mineta, whose breath was wheezing.

There was a chair at the door, where Mineta had tried to open it and get out, but the deadbolt prevented that. The whole kitchen was on fire, blazing up, yet the alarm had not sounded off. Then she remembered taking the batteries out. Mark opened the door, running out of it, not stopping to help Shuga with Mineta.

He dived in his bent-up Cadillac and peeled rubber.

Shuga made it to the door carrying Mineta while screaming for someone to help them. It did not seem to Shuga that Mineta was breathing. Shuga knew nothing about CPR, so she was lost on what to do.

"Nooo!" She did not want her baby to die.

"Nooo!" This could not be real.

"No!" Shuga screamed over and over.

It was like their world had stopped.

Shuga was lost. "Mineta, I love you!" She screamed, telling her for the first time. "Please don't die!"

But right at that moment, Shuga seen as the light was lifted from Mineta's little body.

"Nooooooooooo!"

Mineta never responded.

TO BE CONTINUED…

Text "BOOKS" to 2100 to receive release dates on upcoming books by your favorite author.
Follow on Social Media
IG @redcappublishing
Facebook Red Cap Publishing
Enjoy these types of books look for the following books.

1) "Hard Knock Life" By Tamika Bumpass coming December 2020
2) "Knee Deep In Da Game" By Tamika Bumpass coming December 2020
3) "Life With Louie" By Tamika Bumpass coming early 2021
4) "Sky's Da Limit" Ny Tamika Bumpass coming early 2021

www.ingramcontent.com/pod-product-compliance
Lightning Source LLC
Chambersburg PA
CBHW071517100726
47908CB00004B/1192